Like any ~~~~~~ *~~~~~~*
Dina Dorelli has a few things
to do before her wedding....

1. Figure out whether she even *wants* to get married—'cause right now, she's having some big-time doubts....

2. Convince her old-fashioned Italian family that the night she spent stranded on a mountaintop, alone with a *very* handsome stranger, was completely innocent—even though it wasn't!

3. See the family's new lawyer about getting the prenuptial agreement worked out—and try to ignore the fact that the lawyer just happens to be the same man she spent that not-so-innocent night with!

4. Decide *who* she's going to walk down the aisle with—her same-old-same-old fiancé, or the brand-new man she's head over heels in love with....

Dear Reader,

Only One Groom Allowed. Those words certainly make me think. I mean, really...I don't even have one groom on the horizon, yet Dina Dorelli, the heroine of Laurie Paige's latest, has *two?!* Some things in life just aren't fair, if you ask me. Of course, you didn't. And if I were you, I wouldn't waste time on the question, either; I'd just hurry up and read this delightful book. After all, Dina only gets to end up with one of those potential grooms, and I'm sure you want to see which one.

The One-Week Wife begins Hayley Gardner's duo, FOR BETTER...FOR WORSE...FOR A WEEK! It's incredible to think that a mere seven days can change someone's life so irrevocably—but for the better, I promise you. And after you finish reading Gina and Matt's story, I know you'll want to come back for the companion book, *The One-Week Baby.*

That's it for this month. But after you smile your way through these two titles, don't forget to come back next month for two more books about unexpectedly meeting, dating—and marrying!—Mr. Right.

Enjoy!

Leslie Wainger

Leslie Wainger
Senior Editor and Editorial Coordinator

Please address questions and book requests to:
Silhouette Reader Service
U.S.: 3010 Walden Ave., P.O. Box 1325, Buffalo, NY 14269
Canadian: P.O. Box 609, Fort Erie, Ont. L2A 5X3

LAURIE PAIGE

Only One Groom Allowed

Published by Silhouette Books

America's Publisher of Contemporary Romance

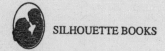

SILHOUETTE BOOKS

RECYCLED PAPER · RECYCLED PAPER ·

ISBN 0-373-52046-8

ONLY ONE GROOM ALLOWED

This edition published by arrangement with Harlequin Books S.A.

® and TM are trademarks of Harlequin Books S.A., used under license.
Trademarks indicated with ® are registered in the United States Patent
and Trademark Office, the Canadian Trade Marks Office and in other
countries.

Printed in U.S.A.

About the author

At our family reunion last year, my sister reminded me that I used to make up stories and insist that she write them down so I could share them with the whole family. The stories were two pages long and involved great adventures that ended when the heroine returned home. "And they were so happy to see her that her mom didn't scold her for being late to dinner," was the way the stories usually ended. She also pointed out that I'm no longer four years old, but I'm still making up stories!

What can I say? I love romance. I rejoice in happy endings. I'm jubilant when they finally say "I do."

Marriage isn't only a grand adventure, but the foundation of civilization. Men would still be living in caves and running around in bearskin rugs if it weren't for women. We bravely confront, tame and soothe the savage beasts...not to mention putting up with whole evenings devoted to channel surfing and toothpaste tubes squeezed in the middle!

Laurie Paige has written over thirty books for Silhouette. Watch for her next story *The Ready-Made Family*, coming from Silhouette Special Edition in July 1997.

Books by Laurie Paige

Silhouette Yours Truly

Christmas Kisses for a Dollar
Only One Groom Allowed

Silhouette Romance

South of the Sun #296
A Tangle of Rainbows #333
A Season for Butterflies #364
Nothing Lost #382
The Sea at Dawn #398
A Season for Homecoming #727
Home Fires Burning Bright #733
Man from the North Country #772
‡*Cara's Beloved* #917
‡*Sally's Beau* #923
‡*Victoria's Conquest* #933
Caleb's Son #994
**A Rogue's Heart* #1013
An Unexpected Delivery #1151

‡ All-American Sweethearts
* Wild River

Silhouette Desire

Gypsy Enchantment #123
Journey to Desire #195
Misty Splendor #304
Golden Promise #404

Silhouette Special Edition

Lover's Choice #170
Man Without a Past #755
**Home for a Wild Heart* #828
**A Place for Eagles* #839
*The Way of a Man #849
*Wild Is the Wind #887
*A River To Cross #910
Molly Darling #1021
Live-In Mom #1077

Silhouette Books

Montana Mavericks

The Once and Future Wife
Father Found

1

Sloan Carradine read the new listing in his appointment book. *Bernardo Dorelli. Prenuptial agreement.*

"Dorelli of Dorelli Dairy," his secretary reminded him. "Mr. Dorelli has a prosperous ranch and commercial dairy business. It's been in operation since gold-mining days."

"Ah, yes, old money," Sloan said, recalling what his two partners, who were also his cousins, had told him of their clients.

"If there's nothing else, I'll be off." Mary cast him a questioning glance.

"That's it. Good night."

When he was alone, his thoughts lingered on the prenuptial agreement. For a moment, memories from the past overtook him. When he'd been six, his mother had left them for another man, trading her family for the love of the moment. She was wed to husband number five at the present.

His grandmother, stern but as steadfast as an oak, had moved into the house to take care of them while his father buried himself in work. From the vantage point of maturity, Sloan understood his mother was like a butterfly, flitting from one flower to another, always restless, always looking for the next thrill, the next grand passion.

His ex-fiancée's main interest had been money. She'd given his ring back and married a man old enough to be her father, one who was several times richer than himself. Then she'd wanted to continue with him.

At twenty-eight, he'd thought his heart was broken for all time. At thirty-three, he knew he'd mistaken desire—a purely physical appetite—for love.

His grandmother had once told him that love was like a tree. It had to be solidly planted in respect and friendship, plus given enough time to form deep roots so it would last a lifetime. Desire was a rose that bloomed passionately and oh, so sweetly, for a season, then was gone.

Live and learn. He had. Desire had no place in a marriage.

Sloan's grip tightened on the appointment book. His client had grown children. Perhaps the man was about to be caught by a fortune hunter, some younger woman who had teased and lured him into proposing. As the older man's attorney, he would write the tightest prenuptial agreement in the history of legal contracts.

Scowling, he put the book in his desk drawer. He decided to drive to the country and stay in the house he'd inherited from his great-uncle for the weekend. His grandfather's brother had been a sharp-witted old gent who had visited Sloan's family in Connecticut occasionally and brought them gifts.

Old Nick had never married, so when he died a few months ago Sloan had inherited a place in the family's Denver law firm if he desired it. His two cousins and he had also received parcels of land. His parcel had been a small ranch with a cabin. Although he'd seized the chance to move to Denver, he was still trying to decide what to do with the ranch.

With a condo in town and much of his time tied up in the city, a mountain retreat seemed a foolish indulgence. He wondered why his uncle had bought it. If the old man had had a family, perhaps a son to teach the fine art of fly-fishing, it might have made sense. As it was, he'd rarely gone there, even after having it remodeled a couple of years ago.

Well, people did foolish things. As an attorney, it was Sloan's job to advise them to think very carefully before they went off the deep end. That's what he would tell Bernardo Dorelli.

Sloan laid the bouquet of flowers on the grass below the headstone belonging to his great-uncle, Nicholas Carradine. He could see why the man had left the family business and moved west to seek his fortune years ago.

Drawing a deep breath of the air, sweet with spring and the promise of summer, he sat on the corner post and let his gaze sweep from one panoramic view to another. From this height, he could see Denver snuggled down at the base of the mountains.

Coming from the East, he had found it odd to be able to see a town laid out like a picnic on the plain. Back East, towns tapered off into suburbs, estates, then small farms with no distinct beginning or end. From here, he could see most of the city, its fringes and the land beyond.

Behind him, like sentinels in white-plumed hats, the snowcapped Rockies stood guard over the plains.

He had located the country cemetery and brought the flowers here at the request of his grandmother who still ruled the family home in Connecticut. It and the small church down the hill were less than three miles from his ranch.

This was the most beautiful spot he'd ever seen. The church custodian maintained the grounds in pristine condition. The peace, the quiet, they soothed the soul—

A voice with the rusty timbre of an old violin rent his contemplation of nature. Snapping around in annoyance, he spied a girl coming up the hill from the parking lot beside the church. She was heading his way.

Damn.

"Climb every mountain," she sang, sounding as croaky as a frog with an interesting case of laryngitis. She paused and lifted her face to the sun, her eyes closed.

His irritation fled as a grin sprang involuntarily to his mouth. She was so obliviously happy, so completely unselfconscious, it was infectious. She was also more than a girl. She was a young woman, her vitality surrounding her with an aura of unbounded, carefree life.

He mentally shook his head at his poetic musing.

He watched her, his curiosity mounting, as she entered the wrought-iron gate and wended her way through the gravestones, studying each one, seemingly searching for a particular name.

She was of average height, but her legs were long and shapely. He knew because he could see every curve in great detail due to the spandex-and-nylon biking pants she wore.

A lot of men were attracted by the feminine bosom— well, so was he, naturally—but he was a leg man first and foremost. Hers were good to look at, gorgeous, in fact.

A T-shirt and jacket covered her body, but when the wind blew the material against her, he could see her derriere was firm and nicely curved and that her waist appeared the same. A nice handful of bosom added to the appeal.

Her hair was black and shiny with just a slight wave. It hung down her back halfway to her waist. The wind tossed it into inviting tangles. He thought of sinking his hands into the silky strands and smoothing them, one by one, preferably across a pillow on the bed in his cabin.

He was rather surprised by the images that dashed through his mind.

After roaming around the lower terraces, the intruder sat on one of the marble markers, crossed her legs and hummed a few notes before breaking into song.

"Down in the valley, valley so low. Hang your head over, hear the wind blow. Hear the wind blow, love..."

The ballad was a perfect choice for that husky cadence. It suited her vocal range. She sang softly, easily, the melody made haunting by the isolated location. The notes wafted up to him on the breeze, intimate, compelling, haunting.

A funny feeling ran down his neck and spine, an electrical tingle that lodged deep within his body. The air, brisk and rather crisp off the mountain, suddenly seemed much warmer.

An answering warmth and a much stronger sensation than a tingle also became noticeable. He glanced down.

It had been a while since he'd reacted so strongly to an unknown female and a rather young one at that. She was probably all of eighteen. He was getting lascivious in his old age.

This wasn't at all like him. He wasn't the type to be taken with a mountain Lolita. He liked his women the way he liked his champagne—cool, sophisticated and not too sweet.

He watched her, unable to look away, while she finished the song, holding the last mournful note until it died away on the wind. Again, a strange sensation ran along his nerves.

She continued her walk among the graves. She hummed along, her voice low and definitely husky.

Rhymes with lusty. Sort of.

Cool it, he ordered his surging hormones. This was not his usual manner with women. After observing his mother and reflecting upon his own love affair, he'd determined to stay in control of his life thereafter—a man who didn't let passion overrule his head. This bit of wisdom had guided his life for the past five years. That one female with a croaky voice could turn him on was a sign that he'd been out of circulation way too long. The fact was, he'd been working hard since moving to Denver a few months ago.

She glanced up the hill and saw him. He witnessed the start of surprise and the flash of wariness in her eyes. He applauded lightly to show he'd enjoyed the entertainment and to indicate he was harmless.

At least, that's the way he hoped he appeared to her considering the state of his body, which was rapidly becoming uncomfortable. There was no way he could risk standing.

"I didn't know anyone was here," she called out defensively, a tinge of annoyance in her tone. Like him, she hadn't liked having her solitude broken.

"I would have called a greeting, but the music was too nice to interrupt." His voice sounded as raspy as hers.

Her eyes were dark and looked black from this distance. Her skin was tawny. A flush highlighted her face, probably induced by the steep climb from the church to the gentler slopes of the old cemetery.

He briefly mused on other things that could cause a flush...all over. He shoved the thought aside.

"Especially when I was caterwauling at the top of my lungs coming up the hill," she added wryly.

Sloan was glad he was sitting down. The sexy huskiness in her voice along with the skin-hugging pants and the wind-tousled hair was a bit...unnerving, to use a mild expression for his reaction to her. He crossed his ankle over his knee and casually rested his forearms on his thighs.

Looking into her face, he was relieved that she was older than he'd first thought. Not by a lot, but some. Maybe mid-twenties. Not that it mattered. He had no intention of getting mixed up with a mountain minx, no matter how sexy she was.

He frowned and tried to get rid of mental pictures of her in his bed, her hair spread over the pillow, gazing into his eyes— He cursed silently.

Dina's first impression was of bigness, as in tall and massive, even though he was sitting. Her unexpected audience was as brawny as a lumberjack. More than six feet, she guessed. Taller than her brothers and most of the men she knew.

Her second impression was of masculine good looks—fit, healthy, tan, with dark blond hair and eyes so blue it was like staring into a late-afternoon sky. He had a broad forehead, an average nose and a firm mouth centered over a square jawline. His gaze was straight-forward and somewhat wary. In fact, he looked definitely uncomfortable as he grimaced and shifted his position.

Of course, he could be freezing his...hmm, masculine

behind off on that granite post where he perched like an eagle, master of all he surveyed.

She suppressed a laugh. This was April in the mountains, and they were six thousand feet above sea level. The wind had a strong nip to it, and the nights could still drop to freezing temperatures. The Rockies were not a gentle place for the careless or ignorant sojourner.

Poor man. She'd probably sounded like a banshee, singing at the top of her lungs as she moseyed through the cemetery, looking at the epitaphs. No wonder he seemed a bit uptight. He might be forgiven for thinking her weird.

She tilted her head to nod to the north. "I live over in the valley. Are you from around here or just passing through?"

"I have a ranch near here."

"The Elk Creek place?" At his nod, she continued, "I heard someone had been seen over there recently, but no one knew what Nicholas Carradine's heirs had done with it."

"It's mine."

Dina heard the coolness in his voice. He didn't like discussing his personal affairs, huh? His smile was distant, too. There was a hint of a frown in his eyes, as if he disliked her on sight. She resisted the urge to ask him really nosy questions just for the heck of it.

"Well, welcome to the neighborhood." She dimmed her grin to a stranger-meeting-stranger smile and decided to head back down the hill to her bike.

"Thank you," he said formally.

A rumble of thunder over a nearby peak heralded her decision as a wise one. She had a fifteen-mile ride back to the ranch and dairy that made up the Dorelli family's livelihood. She was the accountant and general factotum there.

"You'd better keep an eye to the west. There's a storm brewing. See you around," she said cheerfully. "By the way, everyone goes to the Bear Tooth Saloon on Friday night, if you're interested in meeting your neighbors," she added on a determined-to-be-helpful note.

"I may drop in sometime."

When hell freezes over. He wasn't going to be a friendly neighbor. Snooty back-Easterner. "Well, have a nice day."

"Thanks. You, too."

She nodded and turned to leave. She stopped upon noticing the flowers on the grave. "Was Nicholas a relative of yours?"

"Yes." He didn't offer anything else.

Hmm, plays his cards close to the chest, as the cowboys liked to say. Her sympathy cooled. She decided to wait him out and set her face into the most charmingly interested expression she could muster.

"My great-uncle," he finally inserted into the growing silence. A frown nicked a line between his eyebrows.

"You live in Denver?"

"Yes."

"Hmm, your accent sounds sort of back East."

"I'm from Connecticut. I recently moved to Denver to go into law practice with my two cousins." His tone was hard-edged.

"Oh, a lawyer."

"I can see that puts me at the bottom of your social list." His lips curled in sardonic amusement.

"No. Lawyers don't even make the list." She gave him a cheeky grin when he shot her an irritated glance.

She moved up a few steps and peered at his great-uncle's stone. "'To follow the heart is to fully live.' Hmm, I like that. I'll have to remember it for my grandmother. We're looking for something special to go on her tombstone."

He didn't appear quite so formidable when she stood on even ground with him, but he was still big. Size twelve feet. Hands that looked as if they could crush her skull with little effort. However, having grown up with four older brothers, men didn't intimidate her. This one was so attractive she felt in danger of flirting outrageously, though.

Dressed in creased chinos and a white T-shirt under an unbuttoned flannel shirt, he was one heck of a male specimen. Her brothers would be envious of his height, if not his breadth. They were pretty brawny, too.

"I'm sorry," he said.

She wondered if she'd missed something while she'd been admiring his physique. "For what?"

"About your grandmother."

"What about her?"

"About her passing away," he said with ill-concealed exasperation.

"Oh." Dina nearly laughed, but managed not to in view of his temper, which seemed directed at her. "She's not dead yet. She's just getting ready and wants to make sure we don't mess her up."

"She isn't dead?" Sloan repeated. The conversation jumped from one subject to another with nothing in between. He wished she hadn't moved up. The stretchy pants showed off those incredible legs to perfection. He could see every flex and movement as she shifted from one foot to the other. And the way they hugged her as they flowed up that snug seam where her legs joined...

"Nonna is fine. Are you all right?"

No. "Of course." He kept his tone cool. Now if the rest of him would follow suit.

"I promised I'd check out the epitaphs here today. She wants to find just the right one."

"Uh, I see."

"I don't think so," she contradicted. "Well, I'd better be going. That storm is coming on rapidly. I wouldn't stay up here too long. You might get hit by lightning."

He already had, but it had nothing to do with weather. He glanced at the sky. Bright and shining.

"To the west. Our thunderstorms sweep over the mountains from the west. Lots of newcomers don't notice them until it's too late. If you listen, you can hear the thunder before the clouds come over."

"The weatherman said nothing about rain."

"Yeah. They've been wrong before. We might get some hail out of this one. That often happens this time of year. So long. See you around."

Sloan watched as she made her way down the steep part of the slope to the churchyard below and was soon out of sight.

He breathed a sigh of relief. It would be another few minutes before he could stand comfortably, then he could leave. Thunder rumbled, drawing his gaze back to the sky. Yeah, a storm was moving in.

Banishing all thoughts of the sensuous stranger firmly from his mind, he stood and stretched cautiously. Time to get back to the cabin. He'd have a nap, grill a steak and drink a couple of glasses of good wine, then read while the rain pounded on the roof. He started down the steep incline.

The sleet hit his back before he was halfway to the church parking lot.

* * *

Dina scowled fiercely at the flat bike tire, but that didn't do a thing to inflate it. She had nothing with her to fix it, either. Her brother, Joseph, had warned her about riding around the hills without an air pump and tube patch. She sighed. She'd have to push it home.

Unless some Good Samaritan were to come along and offer her a ride. Such as Mr. Grumpy Bear? What the devil *was* his name?

The country bumpkin meets Prince Charming, she sardonically described her reactions. Ah, but he had been handsome.

And about as welcoming as a cat with a tin can tied to its tail. Well, not everyone was as friendly as she was. He'd probably wanted to commune with nature or his past or something like that. Then she'd entered the picture with her singing.

She laughed aloud, but the sound was drowned out by the thunder rolling down the mountains from the peaks. The rain hit the back of her neck at the same time the noise died off.

Sleet.

Just what she needed. She zipped her jacket up to her throat and pulled the hood over her head. There, that would help, but her legs and feet were going to get soaked. In a few minutes, chills shook her as the cold air swept over her and the sun was blotted out by the thunderous clouds.

The sleet changed to minute balls of hail, then back again. Her teeth chattered. The temperature had dropped from crisply pleasant to dangerously chilling in a few minutes.

Ducking her head to keep the sleet off her face as much as possible, she trudged down the road, keeping well to the side in case of traffic. People tended to drive fast in these parts, her brothers among the worst of them.

At that moment, a car whizzed over the rise of the hill behind her and passed within inches. A spray of icy droplets added flecks of mud to her soaked pants.

"Nincompoop," she muttered.

The vehicle, one of those four-wheel-drive yuppie trucks, came to a sliding halt a few yards down the road, then went into reverse. She stopped and watched it powerfully and smoothly zip toward her. The driver was the man from the cemetery.

He stopped and climbed out, his blue eyes causing another kind of chill as they raked over her.

"Hi. Did you come back for another chance to run me over?" she asked, grinning through the icy downpour.

The sleet soaked through his shirt. The flannel clung to him, outlining broad shoulders. "Get in," he said. "I'll put your bike in back."

"That's okay—"

"In," he snapped. He picked the bike up with one hand and headed toward the back of the sports ute.

"Well, since you put it so nicely." She hopped inside the warm interior. Water dripped off her jacket, her nose, the tendrils of hair that had escaped her hood. She carefully pushed the hood off and tried not to sling water all over the leather upholstery.

Looking in the visor mirror, she saw her worst fears had come true. She was about as appealing as a wet cat.

Not that she was trying to attract anyone.

Her savior climbed in.

"By the way, I'm Dina Dor—" The rest of her name was lost in the slam of the door.

"Fasten your seat belt." He snapped his into place.

After she was buckled up, he put the ute into gear and headed down the road. He didn't ask for directions to her home.

"Uh, I was hoping a Good Samaritan would come along," she began after a mile of silence. "I didn't get your name at the cemetery."

"Sloan Carradine."

Her humor faded at the coolness. "You could have told me at the cemetery. Your cousins are our family attorneys—you must be their new partner. No wonder people don't like lawyers. You're so damned sneaky."

He shot her a killer glance before concentrating on the road once more. The sleet and intermittent hail was building up a layer of slush on the blacktop as slick as buttered toffee.

After another mile, he turned off the road onto a gravel driveway. It led to the Elk Creek cabin.

"Uh," she said. "I think I'd better go home."

"You can't. There's an all-points bulletin out from the highway patrol. This freak storm is dangerous. It's already closed the roads farther up the mountains and is dumping about four inches of slush on the area. Everyone is advised to get off the roads and stay off until this is cleared."

"But I only live fifteen miles on the other side of the mountain. I can make it—"

"How? Walking? It would take you the rest of the afternoon and half the night. You'll have to stay here. You can call your folks and tell them you're all right."

"Am I?"

He hit a button and pulled into the garage when the door went up. He killed the engine and turned in the seat to glare at her. "What the hell is that supposed to mean?"

"Nothing. I was just, uh, kidding." She smoothed the wet tendrils around her face. His hard-edged stare bored right through her thinking processes. "Are you suggesting I'll have to spend the night here?"

"No, I'm saying it flat out. You'll have to spend the night here. I'm not driving over any mountain to take you home. I nearly went in a ditch coming down the hill from the church."

Suddenly he seemed much bigger sitting beside her in close quarters. And he looked as if he wanted to choke her on the spot for some strange reason.

"How about if I borrow your ute?"

He snorted and climbed out, leaving the keys in the ignition. She looked at them, then listened to the hail hitting the roof. The sky had turned so dark it was like evening instead of three in the afternoon. She shivered.

The truck door was wrenched open by her host. She jumped down before he jerked her out by the scruff of her neck like an unwanted stray dog. "Thanks so much for your hospitality," she said with a smile. She would be gracious if it killed her.

Of course, he might do that for her.

"Do you hate women in general, or is it just me?" she asked sweetly.

2

Her host stopped abruptly and swung his head around. He raked her with his icy gaze before giving a "huh!" of disdain and throwing open the cabin door.

Dina wondered if that snort meant he did or didn't dislike her. What had she done to tweak his tail, anyway? "I think you dislike women," she said, giving voice to her theory. "That's too bad. Sometimes we're nice to have around. Even my four brothers admit it, and they're first-class louts."

He sent another dark glance her way, then indicated she should follow him. He closed the door behind them.

"Oh, how lovely," she exclaimed.

The room they entered was the living room. It was enclosed by a raised hallway on three sides. The opposite wall contained two doors she assumed were bedrooms. To her left was a bright, modern kitchen. The view from the kitchen was of a patio overlooking a plunge into the valley below.

The living room was furnished with a sectional sofa that formed three sides of a square in front of a free-standing fireplace. The chimney rose straight to the cathedral ceiling and exited through the roof. The skylight at the apex of the ceiling gave a view of treetops and clouds.

"Everything looks new," she commented. "The cabin has been here for about a hundred years."

"It was remodeled," her host said. "This way."

He led her to one of the rooms on the other side of the living room. As she'd suspected, it was a bedroom. The bed was queen-size and covered with an old-fashioned quilt. A padded chair and a table with a lamp occupied one corner. A door opening into the other room disclosed a bathroom.

"Only one bedroom?" she asked, surprised.

"There's another in back that I use." He went to the bathroom door and indicated shelves filled with towels, shampoo and soap. "If you'll give me your clothes—"

Her heart lurched, whether in fright or anticipation, she wasn't sure.

He gave her another of his snarly glances as if he'd read her mind and started over. "If you'll put your clothes outside the door, I'll throw them in the dryer."

"I need to wash the mud out first." She looked at her splattered sneakers and biking tights.

"There's a washing machine. Just leave everything—"

"That's okay. I'll take care of it." She was determined not to bother him more than necessary.

He gave her another glare, then walked out.

She sighed in relief. He was certainly uptight. After closing the bedroom door, she kicked off her shoes and removed her damp clothes. She made a neat stack on top of her shoes and headed for the shower.

Fifteen minutes later, she returned to the bedroom, a towel wrapped around her head, another around her body. She was warm and refreshed. A book, a cup of hot chocolate and she would have been perfectly content. If she'd been at home.

Turning to where she'd left her clothing, she found the pile was gone. Lying across the arm of the chair was a flannel shirt and a pair of tube socks. A blow dryer and comb were on the table. Very thoughtful.

She pulled on the socks, turned them down one roll, then donned the shirt. It smelled of laundry soap and dryer sheets. Since the shirt came down to her knees and the socks came up to them, she was completely covered.

After drying her hair, she sat in the chair and wondered what to do next. She'd have to face him sometime...

She stood and strode toward the door. He might make her a little nervous with his scowls and gruff welcome, but she would not be intimidated by a mere man. She flung open the door.

There was no one in the living room, but a fire was going in the fireplace. She was drawn to it like the proverbial moth.

Standing near the flames, she warmed her backside while she surveyed the kitchen and dining area. From somewhere beyond the kitchen, she could hear the sounds of a washing machine going through the spin cycle. Her clothes, she presumed.

Her host appeared in the kitchen as if by magic. He didn't notice her. She stood quietly and watched him.

He had changed his damp shirt for a dry one. He left it open while he rummaged through the pantry and refrigerator. She watched him empty a can of soup into a pan, then add frozen vegetables, some dried onion flakes, garlic and parsley. He put a pan of frozen brownies out to thaw and made a pot of coffee.

A resourceful albeit reluctant host. That was evident in every stiff line of his massive body, not to mention the dark scowl on his handsome face.

When he turned toward her, her breath caught in her throat. He had showered and shaved since last she saw him. Between the lapels of his open shirt, she could see a rough diamond of brown, curly hair. Beneath the wiry hairs, his skin glowed with a healthy sheen, looking firm and inviting.

She walked into the kitchen and leaned against the counter. From here, she could smell his shampoo and soap. An urge to touch him swept over her, almost over-powering in its need. She couldn't force her gaze from his broad chest, nor her imagination from impressions of what it would feel like to snuggle there, warm and secure from the storm.

At a sound from him, she raised her eyes and met his scorching gaze straight on. He seemed able to read her thoughts. They watched each other without speaking.

She cleared her throat and looked at the hail falling on the stone patio. "Looks like the storm isn't going to let up."

"No." He stirred the pan of soup, then poured two cups of coffee. "I don't have milk. There's sugar if you take it."

"This is fine."

She took the cup from him, careful not to touch his hand. The brew was hot and strong. She'd have preferred cocoa, but beggars can't be choosers, she reminded herself, keeping her gaze from straying his way with an effort.

The kitchen looked like one out of a magazine. The counter was freestanding, forming a U-shaped work surface. Floor-to-ceiling pantries abutted the French doors leading to the patio.

There were no overhead cabinets, so the room had an open, airy feel. A dining table nestled against the left wall. To her right, an open door gave her a glimpse of a huge bed—she wondered if they made special ones for grumpy giants—and another fireplace flanked by easy chairs.

"Very cozy," she murmured before catching herself.

His eyes followed her gaze. He looked from the bedroom to her, then frowned as if he didn't like her seeing his intimate domain. He turned back to his chores.

"You don't have to worry," she advised, irritated by his odd attitude. "I won't attack you while you sleep."

His head snapped up. His eyes blazed over her. "You would be tossed out the door on your backside if you tried it."

She couldn't let that go unchallenged. "Then again, I might not." She gave him a deliberately sexy, confident smile as if positive of her feminine charms. After all, some men did find her attractive, even if this one didn't.

If looks were to go by, she must be on his ten-least-liked-females list. A thought came to her. "Did some woman do you wrong?" she inquired gently. Her brothers always confided in her if their love lives went awry.

"What makes you think that?"

"I thought maybe you'd come to your cabin to get away from all females and, uh, sort of lick your wounds. Instead, here you are—trapped for the night with some weirdo." She flashed him an understanding smile.

"I came here for peace and quiet." His tone clearly stated she was not contributing to the effort.

Well, so much for being a sympathetic listener. "Oh, I need to call my family," she mentioned.

"There's a phone in that wall unit. Pull down the slanted door." He nodded to a cabinet behind the dining table. "There's another in my bedroom if you'd like privacy."

"This will do." She went to the cabinet and opened the door, which formed a shelf for a desk. The phone was inside. She quickly dialed her home. Joseph, her oldest brother, who thought he was boss right after their father, answered.

"Where are you?" he demanded when she identified herself. "Nonna was sure you were dead on the road somewhere."

"I'm, uh, at the old Elk Creek cabin."

"Hey, Nonna, Dina is okay. She's at the old Elk Creek place," her brother yelled. He was silent, then came back on. "She wants to know why you went there."

"It was the closest when the storm hit."

He yelled the news to their grandmother, who, Dina knew, was in the kitchen instructing Lupe, their cook-housekeeper, how to cook Italian instead of Mexican. Lupe had only been with the family for twenty years or so. The two women had an ongoing battle over who was in charge of the kitchen.

"She doesn't like you being there by yourself," Joseph reported.

"I'm not. There's a, umm, the owner happened by and gave me a ride when I got caught in the storm. My bike had a flat."

"I told you to carry the repair kit and pump," her brother reminded her.

"I know. I forgot. Anyway, I'm fine. Tell Nonna and Pop I'll see them in the morning." She glanced at her host. "Probably after church."

Joseph conveyed the information to the kitchen. "Geoffrey doesn't like you missing church. He said his message was especially for you this week."

Geoffrey was her brother, the minister. He was probably in the study working on his sermon.

"Well, it can't be helped," she told Joseph, aware that Sloan Carradine could hear every word she said. Her family could make her feel guilty as sin without the slightest cause. It wasn't her fault that a storm had blown over the mountain in a matter of minutes. "I'll see you tomorrow."

"Don't forget Tony will be here for dinner," he said with heavy portent.

"I won't." She said goodbye and hung up.

"The soup's ready," Sloan announced. He eyed his guest as she returned to the other side of the counter. She was subdued. He guessed her father hadn't liked her staying with a stranger. He ladled out two bowls of soup.

"May I help?" she asked.

"Take the bowls to the table. Why did you tell your father you were with the family attorney? That would have put his mind at ease since we're known to have ice water instead of blood flowing in our veins."

"That was my oldest brother, Joseph. He always tries to boss the rest of us. Do you have ice water in your veins?"

He looked her over. His shirt covered her from neck to knees. She'd rolled the sleeves up to free her hands. The tube socks disappeared under the edge of the shirt. Only her face and hands were visible, but he knew she wore no underwear because they were in the wash with the rest of her clothing.

A sheen of sweat beaded his upper lip. He turned from her and found crackers in the pantry. "Probably," he admitted. "My ex-fiancée thought so." He frowned, angry with himself for that bit of ancient history.

His guest pounced right on it. "She did? When?"

He shrugged. "It was a long time ago."

"Is that why you moved to Denver? Your heart was broken—"

"My heart was not broken," he informed her. "Turns out I was lucky. She married a senior partner in the firm after his wife died. He's old enough to be her father."

"But richer than you?"

"You got it." He smiled to show it didn't matter.

But at the time, it had hurt. He had moved to another law firm to get away from seeing her with the other attorney. Then she'd come to him, wanting to continue their affair.

He had nearly succumbed. Then he'd realized what he was doing. That had cooled his passion and killed any lingering feelings he'd had for her. That had been four years ago.

His Denver cousins had been urging him to join the western firm since Uncle Nick's death. Restless lately, he'd decided to head west, just like his great-uncle had more than sixty years ago, and start fresh.

Glancing at his guest, he smiled. She was bent slightly forward as she carefully placed the bowls of hot soup on the table. The flannel, soft and clingy, outlined her derriere.

The two firmly rounded mounds, the provocative valley between, whetted his imagination and kicked his libido into high gear. He pulled the edges of his shirt together and buttoned it. There. That hid any indiscretion of his from view.

"Would you like a glass of wine?" he asked.

"Yes, please." She retrieved the box of crackers, then waited by the table for him.

He poured two glasses of red wine and took them over. As he drew near, he became acutely aware of her—

of her scent, her warmth, her nearness. After setting the glasses down, he headed out of the room.

"I'll put our clothes in the dryer," he called to her. "Go ahead and start."

In the utility room behind the garage, he threw his shirt, chinos and underclothes along with her shirt, jacket, biking pants and underwear into the dryer and set the machine in motion.

He stayed another moment, aware that their clothing was mingling intimately in the dryer, aware that Dina was in his kitchen wearing his shirt and socks and nothing else, aware that he wanted to mingle intimately with her more than he'd ever wanted anything else in his life.

He couldn't believe his reaction. What had happened to his self-control that this woman should disturb him so?

A shudder of need rippled through him. He grimly ignored it.

She was seated at the table when he returned. She held the wineglass in one hand. The other rested demurely in her lap. She hadn't started eating, but was waiting for him.

He took his usual chair at the end of the table. His foot hit hers. "Sorry. I didn't mean to trample you." Heat traveled in waves up and down his leg. He bit back a groan as the hunger grew to painful proportions.

"It didn't hurt. You're probably not used to sharing the space with anyone."

"That's right. I'm not."

Dina didn't remark on the belligerent undertone in his voice. He was angry again...and spoiling for a fight. She recognized the mood from dealing with her brothers when they were disappointed in life. Usually over a woman.

Her sympathy was aroused once more. "Would you like to talk about it?"

He looked positively shocked. "No!"

She wasn't put off by his snarl. "If you do, I'll be glad to listen. Things sometimes get hard—"

He audibly gulped, choked, then clamped a napkin over his mouth so he wouldn't spew wine across the table.

Dina leapt up and whacked him on the back as he coughed. He was more distressed than she'd thought and obviously still hurt at the breakup with his fiancée. "There, there," she crooned.

"Will you sit down?" he roared when he quit coughing.

She nodded kindly and took her seat without a word. Sometimes it was better to let disappointment fade of its own accord. No unrequited emotion could last forever.

"Once I had a terrible crush on this guy at college. I thought I was madly in love, but I got over it."

"Good for you," he muttered sourly. He picked up his spoon and began to eat the soup.

She did the same. Really, he was quite touchy. Respecting his silence, she ate the meal without another word passing between them. It was a little after five on the stove clock when they finished.

He took their bowls to the sink, rinsed them and stuck them in the dishwasher. All the conveniences of home. Some cabin.

She left him to the chore and wandered into the living room. There, she found a magazine on the outdoors and sat on one end of the sofa near the fire to read it.

Sloan joined her five minutes later. He had a stack of clothes in his hand. "I'll put these in your room." After that, he added logs to the fire and poked it into a merry crackle of flames. He sat opposite her, an oak coffee table between them.

Hail hit the roof with increased force as the wind bore down on the snug house. Dina peered up at the skylight. The sky was really dark now. She could see the tops of trees whipping about in a frenzy.

"I'm glad to be inside," she commented.

He gave his noncommittal little snort.

"Even with a grouch." She realized what she'd said. "I'm sorry. I shouldn't have said that. I'm not normally so rude to the person who rescues me."

Sloan sighed and turned his gaze from the fire to her. "I haven't been a very thoughtful host—"

"Oh, but you have. You've been very kind."

Her face, free of makeup, was smooth and earnest. Her eyes, with the thickest lashes he'd ever seen on anyone, were large and entreating. At the side of her thigh above her knee, two inches of enticing skin showed where the shirt was cut higher and didn't quite meet the top of her socks when she was sitting.

He stood. "I'll see about some coffee and dessert." He headed for the safety of the kitchen and stayed there while the coffee dripped through the grounds. He returned with two mugs and the platter of brownies. He placed them on the low square table within easy reach for her and resumed his seat.

She'd put the magazine aside and was gazing at the fire, her legs drawn up beneath her. She seemed pensive now, dreamy.

Against his will, a vision took shape in his mind like a Polaroid print developing. He saw himself rise and take a seat beside her. She put her head on his shoulder. He held her for a while, then, when she began to stroke her fingers lightly up and down his arm, he drew her to him, kissed her, stroked her, removed the shirt, made love to her there on the sofa in front of the fire...

He hastily downed a gulp of coffee before he did something stupid. It burned all the way to his stomach. He cursed and opened his mouth to let the heat out.

"Did you burn your mouth?" his guest asked.

She dashed to the kitchen and returned with an ice cube and a glass of water. She stuck the ice cube in his mouth when he opened it to tell her he was fine. He took the glass before she tried to pour it down him.

"Thanks," he managed to mumble with a modicum of grace. His eyes were on the level of her hips as she stood over him, her face filled with concern. Her hands on her hips had rucked up the shirt so that a hint of tantalizing flesh was again visible on her thigh. He groaned before he could stop himself.

"You're hurt," she announced with a worried frown. "Stick out your tongue." She bent over. The shirt slid up.

"What for?" he demanded snidely. "Are you going to kiss it all better?"

If she didn't move away, he wouldn't be responsible for his actions. He was losing control. He was...no, dammit, he wasn't. He never lost his head, especially not over a damned woman who was driving him crazy with her innocent concern and gorgeous eyes and legs.

She blinked, then straightened. "Hardly." Her tone had gone frosty. Good, he could use a cold spell. She returned to her seat in a huff. Picking up the magazine, she read it without so much as looking his way for the next two hours. He tried to finish a suspense novel he'd started last night.

Sloan was aware of every minute ticking by. It was now eight. In two more hours, he could go to bed. Not to sleep, though. With his luck, he'd toss and turn all night, thinking of *her* down the hall. An hour crept by. Then another.

He heaved a sigh. When he glanced her way, she was looking at him. She looked away.

"It's ten," he said. He stood abruptly and tossed the book on the table. His body immediately reacted to the idea of going to bed. With her. He banked the fire by pushing cinders over the burnt logs with the poker. Another minute of this torture and he was going to burst into flames right in front of her.

"I think I'll say good-night."

"Good night." He was aware of her standing behind him for a few seconds, as if unsure she should leave. He couldn't face her. He wasn't positive he could keep his hands off her.

"Well, I'll see you in the morning." She padded across the room, stepped up the one step to the upper level and entered the guest bedroom. The door closed behind her.

He heaved a breath of relief, slumped onto the sofa and pressed the heels of his hands against his eyes. He'd developed a pounding headache.

The door opened. He removed his hands and watched warily as she hovered in the doorway. The lamp backlighted her figure, making every curve visible, not blatantly, but enough to whet his appetite for more. He pushed his lips into a smile to allay the startled concern on her face.

"Thank you very much for stopping and for putting me up for the night. And for doing my clothes."

"No problem," he assured her, his calm reply sounding false to his own ears.

She studied him for another second, then closed the door.

He let the fake smile fade and groaned aloud. Ten after ten. The night was going to be a long one. Very, very long.

Dina woke when the sun crested the horizon and shone into the bedroom, its warmth falling across her face like a caress. She watched the valley brighten for a few minutes and mused on her dreams. They'd been confusing, lots of running about to no purpose. But she'd always returned to a cabin in the woods.

Restless, she climbed out of bed. After dressing and making sure the room was neat, she headed for the kitchen. The smell of coffee and bacon greeted her. Her host was up.

She paused at the doorway and watched him. He was turned partially from her as he stood at the stove. His movements were easy. He was obviously a man who knew his way about the kitchen.

Her father and brothers only knew their way to the table. As did Tony Fiobono, her oldest brother's best friend and the man her family wanted her to marry.

Watching Sloan lay slices of bacon on a napkin to drain, she wondered about marriage to a man like him. He was a mystery, someone she hadn't known all her life. He fascinated her with his forbidding scowls and nurturing ways...which he didn't seem aware of. Yes, a very interesting man.

"If you're through lurking, you might set the table," he suggested, glancing over at her.

She started, then grinned. "How did you know I was here?"

Sloan shrugged. How had he known she was there?

Because his personal radar seemed in tune with her every movement. He'd heard the water running in the guest bathroom and known she was up. He'd started breakfast then.

He'd heard her door open a bit later and known she was coming to the kitchen. He'd caught the movement from the corner of his eye when she'd stopped and leaned against the doorway to watch him. Oh, yes, he was aware of her every move.

That acute awareness bothered him. Ha, he mocked himself. Not half as much as his dreams had bothered him last night. He hadn't had *those* kinds of dreams since he'd been nineteen.

He put out plates and mugs on the counter. She carried them to the table. He groaned internally. He didn't know which was worse—having her in his shirt and socks as she'd been last night or seeing her in those leg-hugging biking pants again. Either one was torture.

Clamping his teeth firmly together to hold back a curse, he carefully broke eggs into the skillet. "How do you take your eggs?"

"Over medium."

He carried the skillet to the table and expertly flipped an egg on each plate. She filled the coffee mugs. He returned the skillet to the stove and poured glasses of orange juice. He took them to the table and retrieved a plate of toast from the oven.

"Ready," he announced.

She sat when he did. He was careful to keep his feet in his own space and out of her way. As usual when he was in the house, he was in his socks.

"Good morning," she said in her husky croak of a voice.

He realized he hadn't shown any of the niceties of polite society to his guest. "Good morning."

She looked surprised at the cordiality of his greeting.

He laughed, surprising her further. "I realize I haven't behaved as if I know how to get along in society. I'll try to do better in the future."

"Why?"

He glanced at her, his expression one of rueful amusement.

"I mean, why bother now?" she elaborated. "I'll soon be leaving. If you're lucky, you won't have to speak to me again."

"We're going to be neighbors here in the mountains. And I am a business associate."

"You don't have to worry. My father would keep you on even if I told him you were a bounder and had made a pass at me. He thinks women don't understand business."

"You sound bitter."

She shook her head. "Resigned. Four years of business school, a CPA certificate and he still won't listen to my ideas for the dairy."

"What do you want to do?"

"Get one of the computer financial packages for businesses and bring us into the electronic age."

"Didn't you say you were the accountant?"

She nodded.

"Then do it. That's your domain. You should make the decisions. Of course, you have to stand behind those decisions and admit it if you make a mistake."

"Believe me, my oldest brother would see that I eat crow every day for months."

"Pretty tough, is he?"

"Ivan the Terrible was a wuss by comparison."

Sloan laughed. When she joined in, the merest hint of a dimple appeared near her mouth on the left side. The impulse to lean over and kiss her was powerful. More than that, he wanted to make love to her...

He frowned. These continual sensuous impulses had to stop. No female had ever affected him this way before. Perhaps turning thirty-three reminded him of his own mortality. He'd thought by now he'd have a wife and family. "The slush has melted," he said. "I'll take you home when we finish eating."

Her smile faded. She bent over her plate and ate quickly.

"Not that I'm in any hurry," he heard himself say, "but your folks are probably worrying. My grandmother always stayed awake until I got in from a date even when I was in college and only home for vacations."

"This wasn't a date."

Her flat statement indicated an end to any friendly feelings she might have had toward him. He pushed his plate aside and reached for his cup, irritation at her effect on him overriding his better sense.

"No," he agreed, "but I've wanted you from the moment I saw you wandering around the cemetery, singing at the top of your lungs." He took a drink of coffee.

Her eyelashes flew up. She raised her head and stared at him. "You...you...can't possibly want... You don't...you don't even know me."

"It's quite possible to want a woman without knowing her name or the first thing about her. That's how I felt when I first saw you. And still do," he added with brutal honesty.

"I don't believe you. You haven't acted at all in a...as if you...wanted me." Dina scowled at him. "You've acted as if you disliked me from the first."

The sardonic light in his eyes shook her composure. Having been raised by a father and four older brothers hadn't prepared her for this type of repartee with a male, especially one with Sloan's looks and powerful personality.

"I didn't like having my peace of mind disturbed, not to mention what you were doing to the rest of me."

"It's because of your loneliness," she told him, understanding it all in a flash. "You have this wonderful retreat, and you're all alone."

"Hardly," he broke in.

"Subconsciously," Dina insisted. "I know how the human heart works."

"Yeah. You're so old and experienced."

"I'm twenty-four. That has nothing to do with it. What are you—about forty?"

He shot her an annoyed glance. "Thirty-three."

"Hmm, I thought you were older. You're so stiff and somber and generally off-putting."

"Thanks."

She reached out to him. Laying a hand on his shoulder, she apologized. "I'm sorry. Truly. I know you must be hurting—"

He stood, his chair making a terrible screech on the wood floor. Before she knew what was happening, she was lifted from her seat and caught in the strongest pair of arms she'd ever felt. Her breath stopped as his mouth descended on hers.

She was shocked speechless. And then some.

His lips were moist and warm and demanding. Thoughts of protest hardly formed before they flew right out of her head. He stroked her lips with his, moving first to one side, then the other, as if searching for the best angle.

Wild delight erupted in her. ''Umm,'' she moaned as heat swept through her.

She was lifted and carried, her legs dangling against his, into the living area. There he placed her on the hallway level while he stepped down into the living room. That brought them eye to eye, so to speak.

His mouth continued to ravage hers. His hands stroked along her back. She was aware of his strength, his bigness, the awesome gentleness of his touch. She wrapped her arms around him and clung for dear life, as if she were in danger of being ripped away by a storm tide.

But he was the storm, and she couldn't resist his powerful, tempestuous fury.

When his tongue sought hers, she opened to him, wanting the passionate interplay more than anything.

He ran his hands along her sides, explored the curve of her waist, the shape of her hips, the length of her thighs. He returned to her waist and swept upward. His thumbs caressed her skin near her breasts, creating a rage of heat and longing.

A tremor ran over her and echoed in him.

With one hand, he tugged her hair, tipping her head back. He proceeded to ravish her throat while his thumbs stroked fire into her where he rubbed back and forth, back and forth, lightly, lightly caressing the undersides of her breasts.

She moved restlessly, wanting more, much more from him. She gasped as flames erupted, shooting down to the innermost regions of her body. She protested when he left her lips to slip down her neck to her collarbone.

''Melting,'' she warned. ''I'm melting.''

''I did a long time ago. Yesterday...''

He bent over her, their lower bodies locked together while he strung kisses like pearls along her throat.

"I think I'm going to collapse." She didn't, but her legs trembled, refusing to hold her weight any longer.

He laughed and hauled her against him and carried her to the sofa. There, he laid her down and covered her body with his, fitting them together with careful precision.

As if they were fragile. As if their coming together just so was the most important thing in the world. At that moment, it was.

He sought her mouth again. She met him eagerly, past any modesty or pretenses. There was just him, her and the rush of powerful feelings between them.

When his hand slid under her shirt and closed over her breast, she turned slightly so he could cup her without hindrance. He moved against her, caressing her entire body with his until she felt awash in the tide of passion that joined them.

He released her lips and kissed along her neck, one arm under her, his hand fisted in her hair while the other continued stroking her to a high degree of madness.

She raked her fingers through his hair, each strand like warm silk sliding against her skin. "What are we doing?" she asked, dazed with wonder. "What is this?"

Heat pooled deep in her abdomen. It contracted like a star, growing denser, hotter...

He pulled away from her abruptly. "My God, I'm out of my mind," he said in a hoarse tone.

She gazed up at him, her head still swirling. Slowly, wariness replaced the glow.

He muttered an indistinct curse and turned away. "Madness," he muttered. "This is madness. And it won't happen again." He glared at her. "Do you hear me?"

She nodded.

3

A horn honked outside, breaking the stillness of the moment. Sloan walked to the front door while Dina straightened her T-shirt and stood. Her legs were trembly.

She tried to decide what she felt, but gave up. It was all too confusing and disturbing.

"There's some guy in a black pickup with red pin-striping along the sides coming to the door."

"My brother. Joseph." She ran across the room and stood beside Sloan. "Nonna must have sent him."

Her host went to the door and opened it before Joseph could knock. "Is Dina still here?" he demanded.

Sloan nodded.

"Tell her to get out here, pronto."

Dina grabbed her jacket, went to the door and frowned at her ill-mannered kin. "Allow me to introduce my oldest brother, Joseph," she said with a pointed glance at her sibling. "Joseph, this kind gentleman, who rescued me from the storm, is Sloan Carradine, as in Carradine, Carradine and Carradine, Esquires."

"A lawyer?" Joseph said suspiciously.

"*Our* lawyer, as it were," she announced. She glanced up at Sloan. His blue eyes flicked from Joseph to her and back again, as if looking for similarities.

"Nonna sent me to fetch you home," Joseph informed her as if he expected an argument about it.

"I'm ready. Except for my bike."

"I'll get it." Sloan disappeared into the garage. A second later, the door slid open. He removed the bike from his vehicle and placed it in the back of the pickup. He looked coolly composed.

She wished she could say the same for herself. "Well, goodbye," she said to her host. She held out her hand.

For a second, she thought he was going to ignore her, but then he clasped her hand and shook it twice before letting go.

"Goodbye. Nice to have met you and your brother."

She doubted it, but she didn't say so. She followed her brother to the pickup and climbed in.

"What was that all about?" Joseph demanded as soon as they were off.

"What?"

He flashed her a suspicious once-over. "Anything happen between you two? He try to get fresh or something?"

"Of course not. Sloan is a gentleman, not a barbarian."

"Huh." He took a curve at his usual speed.

"Slow down," she ordered.

He did so fractionally. "Tony will be over for Sunday dinner. He wants to see you. Alone."

Dina tensed all the way from her scalp to her toes. "I'll have to help Lupe."

"After dinner."

"The dishes—"

"Nick can help with the dishes."

"Why Nick? Why not you?"

Joseph heard only what he wanted to hear. "You gonna listen to him?"

"To Tony?" she asked innocently. "Of course."

"None of your smart remarks, either. This is important." He paused. "This kind of thing...makes a man nervous. Don't laugh or anything, okay?"

Dina glanced at her brother in surprise. Joseph, who while visiting relatives in Italy had pushed his way through a crowd of mourners, not realizing their significance until he nearly fell into the coffin, was concerned about another's feelings? Usually her brothers ragged one another and their friends mercilessly over their thwarted love lives.

"I won't laugh," she promised. "But, Joseph, I'm not going to marry Tony."

Her brother's black scowl didn't daunt her.

"I'm not."

"So who do you think is going to have a scrawny chick like you? I don't see men beating a path up the mountain to court you. You'll be twenty-five in another month."

"Thank you for the unqualified praise on my looks," she murmured, exasperated.

"Tony is a good man. He'll take care of you."

"You're concerned about his feelings. What about mine? Don't they count?"

"You don't love him? You've been leading him on?"

She sighed. She'd taken the easy way out and gone to the Bear Tooth Saloon with Tony recently on arranged double dates with her heavy-handed brother. Sometimes it was easier to go along than argue, especially when Geoff joined in with his reasonable tone and logic.

"Of course I haven't led him on. I do love Tony. But

I've known him all my life. There's no fire..." She let the thought trail off.

How could she explain what had happened between her and Sloan Carradine in that strange kiss? She didn't understand it herself. *He* regretted it. She wasn't sure how she felt, except that passion wasn't something she was normally interested in.

"I really hadn't thought about marriage...for me, I mean. You must marry, of course. And Geoffrey, because a minister must have a wife. But Nick and I aren't committed to it." She didn't know about Lucien, her third brother.

"You're a woman," Joseph said as if this settled the argument. "You have to marry."

"Why? Where is it written that a woman must marry?"

"You know what I mean." He flicked her an impatient glance. "Nonna worries about you. You treat all guys like brothers, which is to say, you smart-mouth them like you do me."

Dina shrugged. "If they were really interested, they wouldn't let a little ribbing scare them off."

"Ribbing? You rip their egos to shreds."

"Tough." She laughed at his grimace. "Leave off, big brother. I'm not an old maid, and I'm not a drain on the family. I earn my own way."

"You're not an old maid *yet*. If you wouldn't act so smart—I don't mean play dumb, but tone it down a bit. It makes a guy feel insecure for a woman to be so damned smart."

She held back a scathing comment. Joseph was wonderful at managing the ranch and dairy. He could repair any machine and got along well with their employees, but if he ever felt any of the gentler emotions, he didn't show it. Someday he'd fall in love...and be perfectly miserable, not knowing what had hit him.

"I'll listen to Tony," she promised.

He heaved a sigh of relief and gave her a broad smile. "He'll make you a good husband. He's been in love with you for years, since he was fourteen, I think."

Dina flinched at the thought and felt the weight of someone else's happiness on her shoulders. She did love Tony, but... She just didn't know.

"Go right in, Mr. Dorelli. Mr. Carradine is expecting you."

Sloan stood when he heard his secretary direct his next client into the office. He'd been thinking about this meeting since the weekend.

While the Dorelli Dairy was one of the firm's oldest accounts, he'd gotten over the "nervous suitor" syndrome soon after leaving law school. However, remembering his former fiancée, he was concerned about the older man's marriage.

He went to the door. "Mr. Dorelli. Welcome. I've been looking forward to meeting you."

The man who entered the office was sixty-five, his hair was mostly gray, but he moved with the energy of a much younger man. His handshake was solid, and his whole being was one of sinewy strength. Sloan liked him on sight.

Mr. Dorelli shook hands with him. "I'm happy to do business with you."

"My cousins told me about your ancestors coming west with the Colorado gold rush and starting the dairy business instead of scrambling for mineral wealth. A wise decision."

"Yes. More than a century later, the Dorelli Dairy is

still going strong while the mining moguls are history,"
Mr. Dorelli said with quiet pride.

"Please be seated. What can we do for you today?"

"I want to arrange for my daughter's prenuptial agreement."

Sloan was relieved that the man hadn't fallen for a
gold digger. "Ah, your daughter?"

"Bernardina. She's to marry Tony Fiobono. Fiobono
Cheese," his client declared with a satisfied smile.

"I see." Sloan settled in his chair. There was something about his client that made him uneasy. He couldn't
figure out what it was.

"Dina will receive her mother's jewels upon marriage." Mr. Dorelli drew a paper from his pocket. "This
is the appraisal of the engagement ring and the pearls I
gave her for our twenty-fifth anniversary, plus other, less
expensive pieces. To be fair to all my children, the jewelry must count toward Dina's total inheritance."

"Dina?" A funny sensation hit Sloan in the neck.

"My daughter," Mr. Dorelli clarified. "She's called
Dina in the family."

Like the tumblers in a dead bolt clicking into place,
Sloan locked on to the facts. He looked at the address
on the Dorelli file. It was a small town in the mountains
near the church where he'd met his personal temptress.
Anger simmered in him. "I may have met your daughter. She was caught in the storm—"

Mr. Dorelli chuckled. "Yes. Were you the Good Samaritan who rescued her? We had several laughs while
she told of her troubles. Perhaps she will learn caution
in the future. As a married woman, she will be less impetuous."

"She's agreed to this marriage?"

Shaggy eyebrows, still black as jet, lifted superciliously. "But of course. She has known him all her life. His father is my oldest friend. Tony and my oldest boy, Joseph, have played together since they were children. They, too, are friends."

"I see." Sloan drew a legal pad and pen toward him. "What exactly is the agreement to cover?"

For the next two hours, they discussed trust funds and the amounts of expected inheritances for both Tony and Dina.

"When the papers are ready to be signed, call and I'll have them picked up. We can sign them at the house, yes? Or do they have to be notarized?"

"You'll have to have two witnesses to observe the signing who know the two parties involved either in person or by positive identification. I'll be coming up that way Friday. I can bring the agreement to your place on Saturday and leave them for your daughter and her fiancé to look over. They can mail them to my office after—"

Mr. Dorelli waved aside the delay. "No, no, they will sign on the spot. You can bring them back *subito*."

Sloan cautioned Mr. Dorelli that the Fiobonos should have their own lawyer look over any agreement before it was signed.

Mr. Dorelli waved the notion aside. "We are friends for sixty years. There will be no problem."

And therein lies the fantasy that most people have until the summons is served in a lawsuit. Sloan didn't voice this opinion, but he hoped his client was more astute about his old friend than he was about his daughter.

His lying, two-timing daughter who had looked so innocent, then had kissed him as if there was no tomorrow while planning on marrying another man.

"The agreement is between Dina and Tony, not you and his father," he reminded the older man.

"The children know we will look after their interests. Tony is like one of my own sons. Dina is a daughter to the Fiobonos. There will be no problem," he restated.

The old man's eyes—very like Dina's, Sloan observed, even to the thick lashes—were positive all would be well. He nodded without voicing his doubts. It was, after all, none of his business what his clients did as long as they did it legally.

When the older man left, Sloan stayed at his desk. It was after five, and his cousins would have gone home. He'd like to turn this particular file over to one of them. Swiveling around, he gazed at the snowcapped peaks and thought of last weekend at his cabin, especially Sunday morning.

He wondered if Tony knew his fiancée was one of the most passionate women Sloan had ever kissed.

Of course he did. Nobody got engaged in this day and age without knowing each other in every sense of the word.

A whirl of sensation dropped to the pit of his stomach. He was aware of anger, but the rest he couldn't account for. It was almost like being deceived...or betrayed.

He couldn't think of another word to describe it. Dina had acted the innocent charmer at his cabin. When she'd touched him, patting his shoulder and acting so concerned, he'd lost it. And so had she.

After a second's stiffness, she'd dissolved against him with no protest at all. So maybe she hadn't been as innocent as he'd thought, and maybe he wasn't the biggest cad in the world for taking advantage of her soft heart.

He thumped the pen against his palm and tried to recall how the kiss had come about. He was no longer sure...only that she'd touched him first, then she'd been in his arms, her lips eager for his, her arms wrapped around him, her fingers in his hair, her body under his...

Sweat broke out all over his face.

He swiped it away on his sleeve. The fury gnawed at him. He hadn't known she was engaged at that time, but *she* certainly had.

The first thing Sloan heard on Friday night when he walked into the Bear Tooth Saloon was a choky sound somewhere between a laugh and a gurgle that could have been the muted expirations of a lovesick puma.

It was Dina.

She was on the dance floor, laughing as her partner tried to show her how to do an intricate maneuver that involved holding hands and looping their arms over and about each other in such a way that they came out untangled in the end.

It wasn't working. Instead, the young cowboy—he wore boots, jeans, a silver belt buckle and a snap-front shirt—kept getting them hopelessly tangled up.

On purpose, Sloan decided after watching a couple of tries. He walked over and tapped the guy on the shoulder. "I believe I can be of help."

He slipped between them and took Dina in his arms. He twirled her around, then raised their joined hands and, stepping to the side of her, looped their hands behind their necks, let one hand slide along her arm, caught her hand and twirled her around again, ending with her back to him, their hands still joined. With easy moves, he took them in and out of positions he didn't know he remembered.

"You're marvelous," she exclaimed when the music ended.

He noticed they were the only ones left on the floor. Heat rose up his neck and flowed into his ears.

"When someone is really good or simply feeling feisty, they're given the floor for a number. You were good enough for recognition," she explained.

He followed her to a table, aware that she held his hand and tugged him along behind her.

"Hey, Dina, great dance. When do I get one with him?" a female called out as they passed.

"Come get him next dance," Dina invited.

"Does that mean I've been passed along?" The anger he'd harbored all week resurfaced. He couldn't figure her out.

"Only for one dance." Her rusty gurgle floated over her shoulder. "There are few men who can do more than two-step around here. When we find a good dancer, we share."

"I'm honored," he muttered cynically.

"But only with our close friends," she assured him.

"Thanks."

She looked back at him, laughed, then stopped at a table. The man he'd cut in on was there, along with Dina's brother and another female. The brother didn't speak.

"Joseph," Sloan drawled, sensing the man's dislike and his own reaction to it. He tamped down the male competitive urge and held out a hand. "We meet again."

Joseph stood and shook hands. He introduced his date, Cherry, and his male friend. "This is Tony Fiobono."

"Fiobono Cheese," Sloan said, reminded of the prenuptial agreement. It sounded more like a merger than a marriage. He glanced at Dina, who smiled approvingly at all of them.

Like a mother whose kids were behaving well.

He certainly didn't think of her as a mother figure. While he spoke to the others, he kept remembering the feel of her lithe body in his arms. She'd followed his direction as if they'd been dancing together for years.

"Sloan is our attorney," she explained to Tony and Cherry. "Won't you join us?"

Sloan grabbed an empty chair and set it between Dina and Joseph. They moved to make room for him. Meeting Tony's glance, he saw wariness in the younger man's eyes. Adrenaline surged through him, as if he'd been challenged—

"Beer?" Joseph asked when the barmaid stopped by.

"I think champagne all around is called for."

Four pairs of eyes rounded on him.

"Are we celebrating something?" Dina asked.

"Your engagement." He nodded toward her, then Tony.

The cowboy looked down into his half-empty glass as if embarrassed. Dina frowned. "I'm afraid you're premature. Neither Tony nor I are engaged."

"You've already broken up?" His engagement had been relatively brief, but even it had lasted longer than a week.

"She's thinking about it...about marrying," Joseph broke in with a scowl at Sloan, then Dina.

Sloan studied Tony. The near-fiancé was in his late twenties or early thirties. He had dark hair and eyes and a lean, muscular frame. He wasn't as brawny as Joseph, but he looked fit and clean-cut.

"My dance, I believe," a voice said behind him.

Sloan remembered the dance Dina had promised for him. She introduced him to the woman, whose last name he didn't get.

"Sloan," the woman mused when they took their

place on the crowded floor. "That means warrior in Celtic. Did you know that? Gloria means the fair one."

"Umm," he said. He glanced at the table. Joseph and his date were gone. Presumably they were on the dance floor. Dina bent close to Tony, then nodded as he talked. She laid a hand over his.

Sloan noted the sympathy in her touch, the tenderness in her eyes. The funny mix of sensation hit his stomach again. Tony turned his hand and clasped hers. He brought it to his lips and kissed it, then returned their hands to the table—

Sloan stumbled over his partner.

"Hey, the dance floor is this way," she said in irritation.

"Sorry."

He forced his attention to her. Idly he noted she was lovely, prettier than Dina in a superficial way and with curvier lines. She left him cold.

Clasping her hands, he spun her in a tight circle and lifted his hand over her head so that she nestled beside him, both facing the same direction. He reversed the motion to spin her out, then went through the other steps in his repertoire.

When the number ended, he asked where she was sitting so he could escort her to her table.

"I'm roaming around, talking to friends." She gave him an expectant glance from under her lashes.

He did the gentlemanly thing. "Would you care to join us?"

"I'd love it." Her smile was a come-on.

They threaded their way to the table. Dina looked up from her conversation with Tony. Her expression was solemn.

A slow song started up. "Dance?" Sloan asked her.

He deftly slid his partner into his vacant chair and lifted Dina out of hers with a hand on her arm.

She dropped Tony's hand and came with him. "Was I shanghaied into this?" she asked when he took her into his arms.

He let his eyes feast on her trim form. She wore jeans with high-heeled boots. Her shirt was red with white piping and pearl snaps instead of buttons. At once a vision formed—him pulling the shirt out of her waistband, one good yank and it would open all the way to the top, then he'd ravish her for a bit before slipping it off her, along with her bra...more ravishing...then the rest of her clothing... She'd be busy, too, coaxing him out of his jeans and shirt—

"What?" he asked, realizing she'd said something.

"Are you all right?"

He two-stepped them around the floor, twirled her, then brought her back into his arms.

"No, I'm not all right." He scowled at her. "I'm having a hard time keeping my hands *off* you."

"Your hands aren't *off* me."

"They're not doing all the things I'd like to have them do, either." He gave a sardonic smile as her eyes widened. "Dancing in a crowd hardly counts."

One couple danced by, their arms wrapped solidly around each other, bodies plastered together.

"Now that looks interesting," he drawled. "However, I might not be able to walk off the floor if we danced like that."

"You wouldn't. My brother would beat you up if you tried that with me."

"He might attempt it."

Dina watched his eyes light in amusement. "Men," she complained. "Always spoiling for a fight."

"Yeah, but I'm particular about who I fight with."

His gaze roamed over her, leaving little lightning bolts of pure sensation running over her. It worried her, this man-woman thing between them. He seemed to resent it.

He certainly incited strange feelings in her. Confusing ones, too. She was supposed to be thinking seriously about her future, of falling in love and marrying—

"Why the frown? I didn't step on your foot, did I?"

"No. Can't you tell when you step on someone?"

"Usually," he drawled, "but with a skinny gal like you, I might not notice."

"I'm not skinny," she protested, but not angrily. The way he'd spoken didn't pose an insult. Looking up, she was surprised by the wry half smile on his face. With a start, she realized the light in his eyes was blatant hunger.

"I know." His tone was hard, but sexy, too.

She wasn't sure what to say. He knew exactly what her female attributes were. She couldn't believe he'd held her and kissed her and... Her breasts contracted into points.

His gaze dropped to her chest. He took a deep breath, held it, let it out. When she looked, she saw her nipples were clearly visible against her bra and shirt.

"Yeah, me, too," he murmured, twirling her around and around as the dance ended. He escorted her to the table. "Gloria, how about another go at it?"

The pouty expression disappeared. She smiled radiantly. Dina felt a hitch in her heartbeat when Gloria latched on to him and they returned to the floor.

"Here, Tony, dance with Cherry." Joseph pushed his date at Tony, then took the seat beside Dina.

"Lecture number two thousand and twenty-five," she muttered.

"What's with you and this lawyer guy?"

"Nothing."

"That didn't look like nothing out there on the dance floor. His eyes were all over you."

"Maybe you should insist he wear a blindfold." She smiled, although her body still tingled from contact with Sloan's.

Joseph's face furrowed into worried lines. "Don't let a city dude turn your head, Dina. He's not for you."

"How do you know?"

His scowl softened. He nodded wisely. "Stick with Tony. He'll treat you right."

"No man will treat me wrong. With four brothers, none would dare." She sighed, then smiled. "Let's dance."

Standing, she tugged him to the floor. "Change partners," she called. "Ladies to the right, gents to the left."

She had couples switching partners every sixteen bars of music. There was a lot of laughing and confusion. When she came face-to-face with Gloria, her friend wrinkled her nose. "I'm not dancing with you. I did that at all our high school dances."

Sloan stepped in, took each female by the hand and spun them around. Dina ended with Tony, Sloan with Gloria and Joseph with Cherry. She didn't miss a pointed look from her brother.

Glancing up, she saw Sloan had gotten the message, too. Her brother thought they were with their correct partners.

At midnight, they ordered snacks and fresh drinks. Sloan's leg pressed against Dina's as they all crowded around the small table. Feeling the need for revenge after he'd ignored her the rest of the evening, she rubbed her knee against him.

He stiffened in surprise, then resumed eating a fried cheese stick. She did it again.

"Yes?" he said.

"I didn't say anything." She gave him an innocent glance. She bit into a potato skin. After a few minutes, she rubbed against him again. He ignored her.

It wasn't until she went to the ladies' room that she got her comeuppance. Returning to the saloon's main room, she passed the telephone alcove. She was abruptly pulled into it.

Sloan backed her into a corner and pinned her hands to the wall at her sides. "Now," he said with a moody gleam.

"What are you doing?" she demanded, suddenly breathless.

"Giving you what you've been asking for," he murmured in a husky tone with an undercurrent of threat.

Chills swept over her skin. "I was joking—"

"This isn't a joke."

He took her mouth in a tantalizing kiss that had her trying to get her hands free so she could touch him.

"I'm not letting you go until I'm done with you," he warned, his voice dangerous and sexy.

"I don't want to be free. I want to hold you."

He lifted his head. They gazed at each other, their breathing quick and gasping. "You're an engaged woman."

"I'm not."

"Almost."

She shook her head. "I'm thinking about it to keep my brothers off my back."

"What about Tony?"

"That's the hard part," she confessed. "I've known him all my life. He's a friend and I do love him..."

"But?"

"I'm not sure about marriage." She looked up at Sloan helplessly. "I would like a home and family."

"They usually come with marriage and a husband," he reminded her ruthlessly. "Tony is the only son. He stands to inherit a nice fortune."

She shrugged that aside.

"You aren't interested in money?"

"I can earn my own way. A comfortable amount of money is nice, but it isn't the main thing."

"What is?"

"I'm not sure," she said honestly.

"He can certainly afford to provide you with a home, and he looks virile enough for children."

That made her blush. She couldn't imagine letting Tony do to her what this man had done last Sunday. "This...this is a ridiculous conversation."

"What were you thinking last Sunday when you let me hold you and kiss you?"

"I wasn't thinking at all," she whispered fiercely. She shut up as someone went past the alcove. She doubted they could see her due to Sloan's height and brawny width. "What were you thinking when you started it?"

"I didn't start it. You did," he accused in a low grumble like a storm brewing up in the mountains.

"I did not."

"You touched me first."

She denied it.

"You were all concerned about the state of my heart. You laid a hand on my shoulder."

"Because you seemed sad. An offering of sympathy is not an invitation to grand passion."

"Is that the way you saw it, as a grand passion?"

She couldn't lie. "Wasn't it? One minute, I was feeling sorry for you. The next, I was lying on the sofa. I didn't walk over there," she reminded him hotly.

His gaze burned into hers. "You didn't fight me off. You knew what was happening."

"I was taken by surprise." She decided a good offense was the best defense. "So were you."

"Not exactly." He gave her a ruthless smile. "You must have known what you were doing to me—"

"How should I have known you were having a problem…" She trailed off as his eyes blazed.

"You parade around in front of me all night in my shirt and socks, and yet you have no idea that I might get aroused?"

"It was the next morning, and I was dressed—"

"I'd hardly slept a wink. I heard you in the shower. Then you came out in those damned tight pants."

"That was all I had to wear—"

"They were a red flag to my libido." His jaw clenched and unclenched. "Your father came to the office Monday and had me draw up your prenuptial papers."

"He what?"

"You didn't know?" He eyed her suspiciously.

"Of course not. There's no agreement between me and Tony."

"There is now."

She gazed at him, her expression puzzled.

"Your father had me draw up the papers for you and Tony." He stepped away from her.

"You'll see them tomorrow." He walked into the main room and led Gloria to the dance floor while Dina was still recovering from his news.

4

———— ◄ ————

Dina woke with a headache and an achy feeling all over. Since she didn't drink anything stronger than a glass of wine or a beer occasionally, she couldn't be hung over, but she imagined this might be what it felt like. Glancing at the clock, she saw it was past eight.

She lay in bed and contemplated the sunny day. Even the nearby peaks were free of clouds. It was supposed to be warm.

With a groan, she pushed herself out of bed and into a stinging hot shower. She'd danced the night away, not arriving home until almost three. No wonder she ached.

The tension between her and Sloan could account for the headache. After that kiss and conversation in the alcove, they'd hardly spoken the rest of the evening. But she'd been aware of him. He'd been aware, too, although he'd turned his attentions to Gloria after that. They'd only danced once more, a fast tune that didn't involve touching or talking.

While she was dressing, she heard a car drive up. She went to the window. It was Sloan.

Her heart jumped, then raced.

Strands of honey blond hair lifted and tossed in the breeze when he stepped out of his truck. His eyes were like pieces of fallen sky. He wore an expensive suit, gray with a fleck of blue woven through the material. His tie was a classic paisley in blue, gray and red. It wasn't fair for a man to be so gorgeous.

Resentment boiled in her as she blow-dried her hair. When she tried to braid it, she found her hands were trembling. She used one of her brothers' expressions to vent her irritation.

She was not nervous because Sloan was there, nor because her father had decided to delve into her personal business and have a stupid agreement drawn up. That didn't mean she had to sign the thing. No one could force her. But her hands still shook.

Clipping her hair at the back of her neck with a big yellow bow, she left her room and headed downstairs.

"Dina," her father called as she passed his study, "could you come in here for a moment?"

Her insides tightened to knots. "Of course." She went in, kissed her father's cheek as she had every morning of her life, nodded to Sloan, then helped herself to a carafe of coffee on the credenza. There were also hot breakfast rolls.

"Have you had breakfast?" she asked Sloan politely. "Nonna makes the best cinnamon rolls."

He nodded with stiff formality. "I've eaten, thank you."

She sweetened her coffee, added milk, then took a seat in the other chair facing her father's desk. Joseph walked in unbidden and took up a position near the door.

Like some kind of bodyguard. Her other brothers would have crowded in, too, had they been in the house. If only Nonna, her ally, would come in, but Nonna was in the kitchen, bossing Lupe.

"I have some papers for you to sign," her father began.

Dina took a drink of the hot brew. She hoped it would unknot her insides. "What kind of papers?"

"A prenuptial agreement for you and Tony."

"Would it be permissible for me to see this agreement?" Her father didn't catch the hint of cynicism in her voice, but Sloan did. His eyes flicked to her, and the familiar mocking half smile appeared at the corners of his mouth.

"George Fiobono and I have worked everything out," her father assured her with an airy wave of his hand. "I've read it over. Everything is in order."

"Even the bride and groom?" she asked softly.

"Watch your tone," her brother interjected. A glance from their father silenced him.

Her temper began to fray at the high-handedness of the men in her life. With her father to look after her marriage, Joseph to scold her on her manners and Geoffrey to sermonize about her morals, her life was completely accounted for.

Except for one thing. Her own wishes and desires. She sighed. She wished she knew what they were.

She'd been unsure about marriage before meeting Sloan. She both wanted it and she didn't. If that made any sense. Sharing those wild kisses with the stern attorney had confused her more, preying on her mind constantly during the entire week.

Mr. Dorelli ignored both his children. "Sloan can explain the legal details." He settled back in his chair with his coffee cup and a satisfied expression.

She turned her attention to Sloan. "Do tell all," she invited. His cool disinterest irritated her.

"Why don't you read it first? Then I'll explain any points you want clarified." He handed her a bound set of papers.

Her father frowned at this turn. Surely he hadn't thought she would sign something so important to her future without a glance at it. She pored over every word.

"Very comprehensive," she said when she finished. A cloud of apprehension settled over her. She hated a scene.

"As I told you." Her father smiled.

She tossed the document on the desk and shook her head. "No," she said.

Her father leaned forward. "No, what?"

"No, I will not sign this agreement. I can't," she stated when her father opened his mouth. "I...can't," she finished quietly, knowing her refusal would hurt people she loved.

Joseph broke in. "You said—"

"I said I would listen to Tony. I did. I said I would think about it. I have. I'm not ready to marry. At least, not yet," she added truthfully.

Her father placed both hands on the desk and pushed himself upright. "Not yet? What is this *not yet?* When?"

"When I know what I want."

"You want a home. You want a family," her father told her.

"Well, yes, I do. But I'm not sure who I want to share that home and family with."

"Tony," he told her. "Tony is a good, steady young man. He will bring you much happiness." His earnest smile urged his choice on her. "You will see."

She stared into her cup. She'd explained her feelings very carefully to Tony. He'd understood. "I'm not sure about that. I don't—" She broke off and glanced at Sloan.

He stared at the view outside the windows as if he weren't present. He was probably used to clients yelling at each other while fighting over money and wills and prenuptial agreements. She looked back at her coffee. Resentment of all things male grew in her. They could be so unreasonable.

"You will make up your mind to marry Tony *subito*."

Her father's voice gained an accent as he grew more agitated with his recalcitrant daughter. Dina's heart softened. She hated to disappoint him.

All her life, she'd strived to please her father. He'd been so sad when her mother had died, but he'd comforted his children, each one, day after day until the wounds had healed. She'd been nine at the time. He'd always been there for her. As a child, she would never have argued or disagreed with him. He'd been too important to her world.

She shook her head sadly. "I can't. Don't ask it of me."

He sighed loudly. "It is the way of the young these days," he said to Sloan. "They have no mind for their future." He spoke to her. "A betrothal is a test period, a time for a couple to be alone and speak of their hopes and dreams, to plan together. You do not have to set the date. No, I'm not asking that. But you should use the time to get to know each other."

"I've known Tony all my life."

A dull flush crept into her father's cheeks. "I meant as a man, not as a childhood friend. It is time you stopped treating all men as your brothers. They are not."

Sloan turned from his contemplation of the mountains. His eyes met hers and held. There was knowledge in his gaze that caused heat to gather in her face. She had put that knowledge there with her wild response to his touch. Now, watching him study her, she also saw distrust and a touch of anger. It wasn't a tenth of what she felt.

Her own body had betrayed her, sweeping her into passion so strong she hadn't a defense against it. Sloan must have known the danger inherent in that explosive hunger. He'd been aware of it before she'd realized a need like that could exist between a man and a woman.

"It's his fault," she said, glaring at him.

Her father cast Sloan a perplexed glance. "Sloan?"

"If he hadn't kissed me, I might have agreed to the marriage, not knowing there was anything more than simple pleasure in a kiss, but since last Sunday, I know there is."

Sloan's gaze darkened while resentment blazed in her. She hadn't asked to feel this way...to experience this maddening confusion, this tormenting desire to touch and be touched, but only with one man, only *him.*

Silence fell over the room. Her father placed a hand over his heart. Sardonic laughter gleamed in Sloan's eyes, which also promised retribution. When Joseph started forward, his father quelled him with a glance.

Dina squared her shoulders and faced the men. She knew how Daniel felt when he was thrown in the lion's den.

Mr. Dorelli narrowed his eyes at the attorney. "You will explain this," he said in a deadly quiet voice. "When and where did this happen?"

Sloan met her father's glare with his usual cool composure. "At my cabin. Last Sunday."

The tension climbed several notches. She kept silent, torn between guilt at implicating Sloan in her father's eyes and amusement that he was now on the hot seat, too. That would teach him to be so distant and above it all.

"You took liberties with my daughter by pretending

to offer her shelter from the storm? You took advantage while she was in your home and under your protection?''

At Sloan's annoyed glance her way, amusement won. Dina sat back and enjoyed the drama as her father's indignation grew.

''Hardly,'' Sloan replied, as calm as a Rocky Mountain glacier. ''Ask her what I took that she didn't give freely and of her own choosing.''

Dina sat upright. ''You are no gentleman.''

Sloan smiled in a superior manner.

Her father's outraged countenance switched to her. ''Did you invite his advances?''

''Uh…'' Had she? She hadn't fought him off, but invite…? She wasn't sure. Everything had happened too fast.

''No, she didn't,'' Sloan cut in smoothly. ''It was one of those…spontaneous happenings. However, we both stopped before things got out of hand.''

Her breast tingled and hardened as she recalled how he'd cupped his hand over her. The warmth in her face spread slowly over her entire body. She touched her lips with a finger and recalled how his mouth had felt on hers—the sensuous pressure, the movements, subtle and tantalizing, that had led her down passion's path. She dropped her hand to her lap.

''I didn't object,'' she admitted, her mind going hazy with recollections. ''I don't know how it happened. One minute we were talking, and the next…'' She shook her head, not sure what had happened next.

''Exactly.'' Sloan gave her an oddly penetrating perusal that touched a spark deep inside. It had been the same for him, she realized. He didn't understand what had happened any more than she did. And he liked it even less.

Mr. Dorelli settled back in his chair and studied first one, then the other. "So now you have tasted passion with this man. It began with a kiss, but where does it end? That is the question." He gave them a fierce glance. "Are you prepared to do the honorable thing by my daughter?" he demanded of Sloan.

"Oh, please," she said. The melodrama was becoming too much. "This isn't the dark ages."

The men ignored her.

"And what is that?" Sloan asked her father.

"Marriage."

Dina bolted out of the chair. "You cannot demand such a thing. The kiss was nothing. A moment's madness, that was all."

Mr. Dorelli's expression gentled. He spoke quietly. *"Amore, puo essere la follia dolce."*

She darted a glance at Sloan, but couldn't tell if he'd understood the reference to love being the sweetest madness. "It was not what you say," she replied stiffly. "It was nothing."

She pressed the tips of her fingers together, then spread them like a puff ball exploding to show how fleeting the passion had been between them.

Sloan's tawny brows rose fractionally. His eyes blazed for an instant, then cooled. The hottest flame, she recalled, was the blue one at the tip of the candle.

"I will not be forced to marry anyone," she said with as much dignity as she could muster and walked out.

"Dina," her brother said severely.

"Let her go," Sloan advised.

"Yes," her father agreed in a disappointed voice. "Let her go for now. She will come to her senses soon enough, I think."

Ignoring her father's portentous statement, she

grabbed a jacket and headed for the mountain path and the peace she usually found there.

The soft knock on her door preceded the entry of Dina's grandmother into her bedroom. The tiny wizened lady carried a cup of hot chocolate.

"Nonna, how thoughtful," Dina murmured. She dredged a smile to her reluctant lips.

"I saw your light still on and knew you couldn't sleep." Nonna handed the cup over, then sat on the foot of the bed, her eyes, set deep in their sockets, belied her ninety-three years with their alert awareness. "It is very hard to go against the wishes of the parents, eh?"

Dina nodded. "Papa thinks he knows best for me, but... I feel like a terrible ingrate, making him angry and...and also disappointing him. He thinks of Tony as a son."

"The boy has grown up in this house as much as his own. As you have in his."

"I know."

"Have you talked to him?" Nonna smoothed her apron over her black skirt, then rolled her hands in it as if to keep them warm.

Dina had seen the gesture thousands of times. It meant her grandmother was troubled.

"To Tony? *Gia.* He understands."

"What are his feelings?"

"He says he has loved me since we were children and always assumed that we would wed someday." Dina gave her grandmother a troubled glance before sipping the soothing drink.

"And you hate to hurt him," Nonna concluded, understanding her feelings exactly. "A woman's heart is soft, but now I think yours needs to be strong." The older woman again smoothed her apron, then pulled the hem over her hands.

Dina waited.

"I will tell you a story. When I was a girl, younger than you are now, and oh so eager for life, a man came to our village. He was thought to be rich. By our standards, he was. This was a mountain village, you understand, and a poor one."

"*Sì*," Dina murmured, encouraging Nonna to continue.

"I fell in love and wanted to marry him, but my father said no. This was not the man for me. He arranged for my betrothal to another."

"You agreed?"

"*Sì*. I am like you, confused by the heart. *Caspita*, so confused. I trusted my father, but I was unhappy and afraid of making the big mistake, you understand."

"So you did not marry either one," Dina concluded.

"But yes." Nonna's eyes lit up. "On the night before he left, our visitor came to me. He said he could not live without me. He wanted me to come to America and be his wife."

Dina blinked in surprise. "It was Grandfather?"

"*Sì*. He kissed me, and I am...transported?"

"That about describes it," Dina agreed wryly, thinking of Sloan's kisses.

"He asked if I am sure and if I can be strong enough to face my family. I say yes. So your nonno woke my father and they have the, um, *uomo a uomo*, you understand."

"Man-to-man talk, *sì*."

"There was much shouting and arguing in the family, but I hold firm and so does my lover. And so we win in the end. I came to this country a year later."

"A year?"

"My father insisted we must write and know each other. We do, and we send pictures. I fall in love with the mountains before I arrive. They are like my village. And so I have been content here in this country."

"You followed your heart," Dina said softly. "Oh, that reminds me. How do you like this—'to follow the heart is to fully live'? I saw it on Sloan's great-uncle's headstone."

"I will keep it in mind. Write it down on our list in the morning."

"I will."

The gnarled hands came out from the apron and clasped Dina's face. "Promise, no matter what my son says, that you will follow your heart. He married your mother without knowing her for more than a week." Nonna smiled like a mischievous leprechaun. "But of course, she was another man's daughter."

"But, Nonna, I don't know where my heart is leading. I think it's going around in circles."

"I think your heart is pulled too many ways by those who have not the right. Do not do anything foolish." She kissed Dina on each cheek, took the empty cup and silently left the room.

Dina leaned back on the pillows. It was odd to think of her grandparents as impetuous young people who defied her family to marry. And her parents, marrying after only a week. That was the most shocking fact of all, one her father hadn't seen fit to mention to his children.

A knock interrupted her musing. "Come in."

Her youngest brother, Nick, slipped into the room. He was sixteen months older and the one she was closest to. He had two cups of chocolate and a plate of cinnamon rolls on a tray.

"I thought Nonna would never go to bed tonight. She just now went to her room." He eased the door closed.

Dina nodded. "She stopped by here." She took the mug of cocoa he offered and sipped from it. She declined a roll.

"Joe was ranting and raving about what happened. He said you were being stubborn and foolish. As usual." Nick grinned.

She huffed in exasperation. "I wish the men in this family would let me make my own decisions."

"Such as who you should marry? Have you gone off the deep end over this lawyer guy?"

Catching his sleeve, she gave it a yank. "Not you, too." She set the cocoa aside, sighed and folded her arms around her drawn-up knees.

"Sorry. That was Joe's version. I'm here to listen to yours if you want to share it."

"I have a question."

"Shoot."

"You've been in love…" She hesitated. Her brother's affair had ended badly. She didn't want to remind him of it but she needed his advice. "Have you ever been in love?"

"Yes."

"How did you feel?"

"It was hell." His eyes darkened. "It still is," he concluded.

"You still love her," Dina concluded breathlessly. "After all this time?"

"No," he denied, a trace of bitterness in the word.

"Oh, *caro mio*—"

"Don't go smarmy on me." He gave her a stern look. "It isn't my love life that's in question here. What happened to you and this lawyer Joseph wants us to knock around a little bit—''

"Don't you dare!"

Nick grinned and held up his hand as if to ward off blows. "We won't." He sobered. "Are you in love with him?"

"No. Not at all." She leaned her head to one side and considered. "I don't think. I mean, this can't be love— this ridiculous yearning to rip his clothes off and have my way with him, can it?"

"Holy moly," he said in mock concern. His gaze went solemn. "That is one of the signs."

Dina sighed. "I can't marry Tony when I go all trembly at the touch of another man. It wouldn't be fair."

"Damned right it wouldn't."

"So what do I do?"

"Get over this Carradine guy first. And make damned sure you are over him before you go to anyone else."

"How?"

Nick shook his head. "Only you can answer that."

"Maybe I should have an affair with him," she mused. She started laughing. Nick knew her views on that.

"Yeah." He pulled her hair, then drank the rest of her cocoa and stood. "I'd better be going. By the way, I think Dad is up to something. He and Nonna were talking, but shut up when I appeared. Watch your back," he advised with a wry grin.

She rolled her eyes. "Why was I born into a nosy Italian-American family?"

"Just lucky, huh?"

Dina rose to her knees and gave him a hug. He'd had his share of questions from their father about his future, too. He'd fought hard against joining the family business to become a cop. It was what he'd always wanted.

After Nick left, she turned off her light before Joe or Geoff or Luke felt duty-bound to barge in and advise her.

Settled under the comforter, she began to drift off when she had a vision of another bed. She was snug in it. A fire crackled on the hearth, making cover unnecessary. She was wearing a pair of slinky lounging pajamas...which she didn't own.

A man came into the room. He was magnificently nude.

"Blond all over," she murmured.

Every muscle in her body jerked, almost throwing her out of bed. Her eyes snapped open to their widest. Never had she had such thoughts, such lascivious images, never.

She didn't know what was happening to her. Sighing, she punched the pillow and turned on her side. She'd sing songs until she went to sleep. Ah, that old Everley Brothers ballad. *Dream, dream, dream...*

She did. All night. She woke more exhausted the next morning than the previous day. Sloan Carradine had invaded her mind. What was she going to do about him?

Wed him and bed him, suggested a part of her that was sly and tricky and entirely untrustworthy.

"Enough," she ordered and headed for the shower.

The first person she saw at church, besides her family, was Sloan. He was standing on the porch beside her brother, who was the minister at the small, nondenominational church.

There was a general round of greetings from everyone. Nonna held her back when she would have gone in. Dina gave her a questioning glance, but Nonna only smiled.

"May I join you?" Sloan asked.

"Yes," Nonna replied. She took his arm and nearly pulled him inside to their pew. That left Dina to follow alone. It also meant she had to sit by Sloan at the end of the bench.

The hour went by swiftly. She listened to every word of the sermon, sternly keeping her mind disciplined. At the close, Sloan held the songbook for her and Nonna, and the three of them sang from it. He surprised them by singing harmony with Dina.

"You are good together. Perhaps you should do a duet," Nonna suggested while they waited their turn to file out.

"No one wants to have to listen to me," Dina protested, grinning. She knew what she sounded like.

"You have a good alto voice," Sloan said. "It could be trained if you wanted to increase your range."

"There's no one around here."

"There is in Denver."

"That's too far."

"It's hardly more than an hour's drive. Your father said you play the guitar. How did you learn?"

"Nonna taught me."

He turned to the tiny wisp of a woman. "Your talents amaze me. Dina said you baked the rolls your son sent home with me. I had them for breakfast."

Nonna nodded her head several times, pleased at the compliments. "Dina is equally at home in the kitchen."

"I'll have to remember that," he murmured before stopping to speak to Geoffrey.

"He is a big man," Nonna said in Italian as she and

Dina continued outside. "Did you notice the size of his thumbs? A virile man. He will produce fine babies."

"Nonna!" Dina looked back over her shoulder, but Sloan was shaking hands with her brother. Thank goodness he hadn't heard. "That's just an old wives' tale."

Nonna cackled softly.

Dina had to grin. "Be careful that you don't lay an egg."

"Be careful that you don't mislay your heart."

By one, the clan had gathered at Dina's house for Sunday dinner. Besides her immediate family, her aunt and uncle, who were sister and brother to her father, were present along with their spouses and sons, Dina's five male cousins. Her father had also invited Miss Pettibone, a spinster who'd been with the dairy for centuries, according to her brothers.

Dina greeted the older woman, who then hurried to the kitchen to help Lupe.

"Ah, here she is," her uncle said, beaming and patting both her cheeks when he came in. His mood was expansive. "Your papa did well for you, yes? Everything is arranged nicely?"

Her father met her startled gaze. She realized he'd told his brother of the marriage without consulting her. A strange ache settled somewhere inside her near her heart. Everyone knew her business but her.

"There is no arrangement," her father said, his anger with her stubborn foolishness obvious.

Her aunt exclaimed softly and mournfully, then gave her a kiss on the cheek when the older brother and his wife moved on. "Don't worry," she advised. "Tony will come around."

Dina shook her head. "It isn't Tony. I'm not ready for marriage, but father insists."

"He wants you married and with children. It was the same with my father when I was young." She gave a helpless sigh.

"He won't listen when I try to explain," Dina said.

"Your father is a stubborn man."

"Then I come by the trait honestly?" she inquired mockingly.

Her aunt Rosie patted her cheek. "Men don't understand that it is the woman who decides upon the marriage. When you are ready, you will know."

Her aunt laughed and went to the kitchen to greet Nonna and Lupe and Miss Pettibone. Dina set the table, recalling all the times she'd listened in on her brothers' discussions of girls without their knowing it. Then one day, they'd caught her with her ear to the furnace register in her room, avidly gleaning all their youthful secrets and opinions on women.

Her cousins drifted by, their greetings affectionate and teasing, their glances speculative.

As usual, the entire family knew everyone else's personal concerns. She sighed and folded the linen napkins into swan shapes before placing them on each plate. The doorbell rang. She paused and listened to discover who else had arrived. She hoped it wasn't Tony and his father. She didn't want to face Mr. Fiobono.

She heard a smooth baritone answer her father's greeting. Her heart lurched, then beat like mad. It was Sloan.

She went to the archway between rooms. Sloan had removed his jacket, but otherwise was dressed in his church clothes. His smile changed when their eyes met. She felt a deepening inside as if something unknown wavered, then expanded.

"Are you joining us for dinner?" she asked him. She cleared the huskiness from her throat.

"Yes. Your father asked me."

Neither of them offered a hand to the other. She drew a shaky breath when he walked by and spoke to her brothers, one by one. She felt fragile inside, as if her heart were made of the thinnest crystal.

It was strange. No matter how she tried, she couldn't account for the way Sloan made her feel. Each time she met him, she grew more and more confused. She hurried to the kitchen.

"More garlic," Nonna said to Lupe, a spoon in her hand.

Lupe snatched the spoon from her and stirred the contents of a skillet. "It has more than enough."

"Let me taste," Dina offered. "Enough," she agreed with Lupe, who beamed while Nonna frowned. Miss Pettibone and the two aunts hid their smiles.

"I want you to make the pastries for my wake," Nonna told Dina with a glare at Lupe. "Lupe always gets them wrong."

"I will," Dina promised.

Nonna went to check the table. With a houseful of family to feed, the older woman was in heaven, and her temper was soon restored. After everyone was gathered and Geoffrey had said the blessing, Nonna indicated Sloan was to sit next to Dina. Her dark eyes sparkled happily. Dina's father smiled benignly.

A frisson swept over Dina. Something was out of kilter here. She had a feeling she'd soon know what.

5

During the meal of spring lamb with new peas, polenta tarts, garlic squash, angel-hair pasta with sun-dried tomatoes and Nonna's delicious homemade rolls, Dina stayed alert to subtle nuances in her father's surprisingly jovial manner. He wasn't a man to carry a grudge, but neither did he relent readily once he made up his mind.

Later, eating dessert, she became aware of Sloan's speculative gaze on her as he observed her and her family with that distant courtesy lawyers were so good at. She had to admit he had charmed the family in the best way possible—by listening attentively to their anecdotes.

After Aunt Rosie, her father's sister, related a humorous incident concerning her two grandsons, Dina's father said he was going to give up on having grandchildren if one of his children didn't marry soon. His gaze settled sternly on her. Everyone else followed suit.

Dina felt the weight of her entire family's expectations squarely upon her shoulders. The rebellious instincts she'd buried years ago resurfaced. No one hounded her brothers about marrying and producing children, and they were all older than she was. She returned her father's stare with a stolid expression of her own. Beside her, Sloan stirred as if he might say something to break the tense silence.

For a heartbeat, she considered what would happen if he suddenly declared to her father that she couldn't marry another, that they belonged together. The thought was gone in another instant. Reality returned.

She finished the meal without taking part in the general discussion. Her awareness of Sloan was so intense, she felt as if electric currents raced along her side. She thought of Tony. He was her oldest friend. A marriage between friends had to be more lasting than passion between strangers.

Finally the men retired to the living room. The women cleared the table and talked of things close to their hearts.

"Callie has gained thirty pounds," Aunt Lerna, wife to Uncle Bert, related. "The doctor says it is all right, but I tell her every pound over twenty will stay on her."

Babies, Dina mused. Marriage and babies and family, that was all they talked about. Men talked of weather, livestock and crops. And sports, she added, hearing her brothers and cousins arguing whether a batter was out or safe.

"Dina," her father called to her. "Sloan would like to see our operation. Perhaps you would give him a tour?"

Her earlier wariness revived at this request. Her father was very proud of the dairy and the family traditions behind it. Normally he would give the tour himself. This was no spur-of-the-moment idea. She knew her father too well for that. He was sending her off with Sloan for reasons of his own.

"Of course." She wanted to get away from the talk of babies and husbands…and find out what her father had up his sleeve.

"Go, go," Nonna urged, pushing her from the kitchen.

"I'll need to change." She glanced at Sloan.

"I have clothes in my car." His expression was unreadable.

Dina went to her room. Her hands trembled as she changed to jeans and a cotton sweater, then laced up her sneakers. Their guest was ready and dressed similarly when she returned.

"Ready?"

"Yes." Sloan didn't normally intervene in his clients' affairs, but he felt obligated in this case. Because of one ill-advised, unplanned kiss.

Impulsive behavior wasn't at all like him. If he hadn't given in to that insanity, Dina would probably be engaged and happily planning her wedding by now. Certainly she had been considering it. Until the fateful kiss. So it was up to him to help rectify the situation. After all, he was the one who believed that marriage should come from a deep, abiding friendship, not the blinding passion he had with Dina.

At any rate, her father had said he would disown her if she didn't come to her senses soon. Now that the time had come, he wished he hadn't succumbed to Mr. Dorelli's entreaties....

"She will listen to you." The old man had put a hand to his heart. "Tell her I am going to change my will."

Sloan had pointed out the split in the family that would most likely result from such action, but Mr. Dorelli had remained adamant. His daughter was being stubborn. She needed a push in the right direction. He had forgiven Sloan the indiscretion of the kiss.

"She would miss her family very much if you forced her to leave," Sloan had reminded the older man.

"If she leaves, I will leave, too," Nonna had spoken up, coming into the room and giving her son a harsh glance. She laid a hand on Sloan's arm. "Talk to her," Nonna had urged.

"I'm sure I have no influence—"

"More than you know, I think," the old lady insisted.

"Come to dinner tomorrow," Mr. Dorelli said. "That will be the best time to talk."

"Yes, after church. One o'clock," the grandmother seconded.

Sloan found himself agreeing to the mission. So here he was. He experienced a leap of his pulse when Dina led the way out. He quelled it ruthlessly.

"Go on with you." Nonna pushed them toward the door.

The tour of the immaculately clean dairy operation took thirty minutes. Dina explained how the milk was pasteurized in huge stainless-steel vats. "The cream is siphoned off here." She pointed out the glass pipelines that moved the milk from one operation to another. Last, she showed him the Spartan offices where the business was conducted. Her office was the only one with lots of plants and colorful prints. Miss Pettibone, the book-keeper, did keep a row of violets on her windowsill.

"Would you like to see the dairy herd we keep?" she asked when they left the building. "It's up a rather steep ridge, but you'll get a wonderful view of the valley."

"Yes." Sloan rehearsed several openings concerning her future on the way up the ridge. By the time he reached the peak, he'd discarded all of them. He shaded his eyes with one hand while he surveyed the rocky out-cropping ahead of them.

His escort wasn't breathing hard. She was in good shape in more ways than one. The blood pounded in his body as he watched her climb the narrow trail in front of him.

"This is one of my favorite places," she told him when they got to the top. She took a seat in a hollow formed by the granite boulders.

She'd tied her jacket around her shoulders by the sleeves. The light fragrance of her perfume teased his nostrils. It had nearly driven him mad during the church service. He beat back his libido by sheer dint of will. He had a duty to perform.

He took a seat on the rocky shelf beside her and made a cushion of his jacket for his back.

"Ah, life as it was meant to be lived," he murmured. "What a view. It may be better than the one at the cemetery."

"You traitor," she said.

"I beg your pardon?"

"I finally caught on when I was asked to give you the grand tour. My father wants you to talk to me." She gave him a glance of purest contempt before looking away.

Sloan held on to the fine edge of control he maintained in all his dealings with clients. "That's hardly a traitorous act. I'm here *pro bono,* that is, for the common good. Think of me as a friend of the family."

"Ha."

With Dina, he needed as much control as he could muster. Sitting beside her, protected from the wind and warmed by the sun, a man could easily be lulled into a false security.

"You're here at my father's request—"

"Actually, your grandmother's."

"Nonna?" She thought about this. "Why?"

He let Dina stew over the situation before he spoke.

He wanted her relaxed and off-guard. He used the time to view the Dorelli ranch below them. A small creek threaded its way along the narrow valley. Black-and-white cows grazed in the pastures, which ran up the shoulders of the hills. Dorelli Dairy was written on a large white building that faced the county road. Tank trunks were visible through the open bay of a parking barn.

"Do you go out to the ranches that have dairy herds and collect the milk?"

"Yes."

"How do you get through winter blizzards?"

"The county keeps the roads open. The valley is in the rain-shadow of the mountain. We get mostly melt and runoff rather than snow. We move our herd to the lower pastures and feed them hay during the winter."

He was aware of her breasts lifting as she drew a deep breath and let it out in a sigh. She had the sweetest scent, light and sultry. There, just below her ear was the softest place. He wanted to taste her—

Damn. He was forgetting why he was there. He had to maintain a…a paternal attitude. He was, after all, a stand-in for her father. "Your father wants what's best for you," he began. He realized he sounded as patronizing as a judge he'd once known.

"What he thinks is best, not what I think is best." She spoke without heat. The anger was gone, leaving a stubborn resignation in its stead.

His own curiosity prodded him to ask, "Why haven't you married before now?"

She shrugged.

"You're too passionate a woman to remain alone." The words were out before he could stop them.

"Sex?" She gave a snort. "I can live without it."

He thought of her mouth and the way she'd opened to him, moist and sweet and welcoming. "You came apart in my arms when we kissed."

"That was a mistake."

Sloan was taken aback at the flat statement. He'd planned to convince her of that very thing, then turn the conversation to yesterday's contretemps with her father. Instead of being pleased, he found himself wanting to argue the point.

Ignoring his personal feelings, he continued the debate. "Tony seems to truly care for you."

"Of course he does," she said, as if it was too obvious to mention.

"He'll take care of you. You have a common background and a long history. It would be a good match," he recounted what her father had told him and his own impressions of the younger man from Friday night.

She turned a frigid gaze on him. "I don't want to be taken care of."

"What do you want?" It was often effective to turn the opponent's reasoning around and use it against the person.

Instead of answering, she dropped her head forward and peered at the ground between her feet. Her hair fell to the side, exposing her nape. It looked...kissable.

"I don't know." Misery seeped through the admission. "But I won't be part of a business merger. Our fathers can have that without involving me and Tony."

He reached out to smooth the tangles of hair that had escaped the barrette and nearly touched her before he caught himself. The anger he'd felt since he'd written the prenuptial agreement surfaced. He was here as the devil's advocate, a spokesman for the family. He had to keep his hands off her.

"Are you being fair to Tony or yourself?"

She raised her head. "What do you mean?"

"I think you have the best basis for marriage of any couple I've met. It's obvious you two are the best of friends and that there's a great deal of affection between you."

"Is that enough?" She sounded so miserable, he wanted to comfort her. He saw in her his younger, idealistic self, when he'd thought a fleeting passion was the love of his life.

"Yes. Don't let the fire that ignited between us confuse you. It was an aberration of the moment."

"How did you feel when you fell in love?"

"My experience was hardly one to go by."

"True. You haven't done any better than I have in finding your true love, but you must have felt something different from what you felt for other women. Did you share a grand passion? Were you friends before you fell in love?"

"We were never friends. She was a tease. She knew every trick in the book to make a man think he had to have her."

"Did you? Have her, that is?"

He gave her a stony glare.

"I tried sex once," she confided in a musing tone as if recalling a bad dream.

Sloan recalled she'd confessed to having a crush on someone during her college days. Surely she didn't mean what he thought she meant. "Once, as in one affair, or...once, as in one time?"

"One time. I have to tell you, I don't see what all the fuss is about—"

He choked on this piece of news.

She watched him in concern.

"Bungler," he muttered.

"What?"

"To be given the gift of a woman's passion, then to bungle it, is inexcusable," he said, anger roiling in him. He touched her face, which was hot. He realized she was embarrassed. An incredible tenderness shot through him. "You found the experience embarrassing. Was it also unpleasant?"

"Actually...yes."

"It doesn't have to be like that." He ran his fingertips over her cheek. Her skin was incredibly smooth. "Remember when we kissed? You wanted more then."

She studied him, her expression confused and worried. "That was different. It was kissing and caressing, not sex."

"It would have been. That was the next step...to go all the way with each other. We both wanted it."

"I didn't—"

"Yes," he interrupted. "You just didn't know it."

"Please don't start telling me what I want. I get enough of that at home."

He picked up a strand of her hair and smoothed it around his finger. The need to touch her was overpowering. He squelched the fire inside. He had to stay in control. He was here on a mission for his client.

She pulled away. "Don't."

"Why so touchy today?"

"I'm angry with you. You drew up that agreement."

"I didn't know you were opposed to it at the time."

"You're here at my family's request to talk some sense into me, using your lawyer's logic to convince me I'm wrong." She faced him. "How can you encourage me to go to Tony after what happened between us?"

"Nothing happened between us." He tried to sound

wise and reasonable about the whole thing between them. "That is, there's an explanation. I've been busy, under a lot of pressure at work, you were being pressured by your family, we were trapped together by the storm, the rest was proximity. I was attracted. So were you." He shrugged to show it meant nothing.

"Two lonely lambs ready for the shearing," she mocked.

"Women react emotionally to life. The passion confused you. You think it has to signify love. It doesn't."

"I never said that."

"You're thinking it. I could make love to you right here, right now. It wouldn't mean a thing, except a physical attraction. Passion is fleeting. Marriage needs a firm basis, such as the friendship you share with Tony." He lifted the strand of hair.

She pulled the curl from his hand. "Maybe I should have two husbands, one for passion and one for friendship."

He smiled at her churlish suggestion. "Sorry. Only one husband allowed...at a time, that is."

"Are all lawyers pompous asses?"

He chuckled, knowing his calm logic had penetrated her defenses. People resorted to insults only when they weren't winning the argument. He had done his job well. "Just the ones you know."

"Yeah. Okay, you've done your duty. You can leave now."

"Now, now," he chided with expansive cheer. "That isn't very friendly to someone new in the neighborhood."

"Or you can kiss me," she added when he didn't go.

Hmm. A direct challenge. He would ignore it, of

course. He had the upper hand. To stay longer would be to gloat.

She flashed him another defiant glare.

He paused. She probably didn't even realize she was daring him to kiss her. He should ignore her little feminine ploy—

Giving a disdainful snort, she tossed her tangled hair over her shoulder as if throwing down the gauntlet.

That did it. He pulled her into his arms. He paused with his mouth a hair's width from hers. "Passion is a mindless need that has nothing to do with love."

"Are you doing this to prove your point?" She didn't flinch or try to pull away.

With a startled insight, he realized he wanted to be the one to show her what passion was really about... what it could really be between a man and a woman. So much for his paternalistic, I-know-what's-best-for-you attitude.

"Hell's bells," he muttered. Releasing her, he stomped down the mountain before he forgot all sense of propriety.

Sloan smiled absently at his date, glad he'd let his cousin talk him into it. The evening had turned out pleasant enough, and he'd needed the distraction. She raised her finely arched eyebrows. He realized she'd asked him a question and was waiting for his reply.

"I'm sorry. I was thinking of a, um, legal brief," he said. Yeah, right. He'd been thinking of a certain mountain minx who haunted his dreams. His emotions alternated between cynical amusement and raging lust for her.

As a man who prided himself on his good sense, he

was angry with himself that he seemed to have so little when it came to thoughts of Dina Dorelli.

"Well?" his date said.

He realized she'd asked her question again. He hadn't heard a word. Damn.

Taking himself firmly in hand, he set out to charm the friend who was visiting his cousin's wife. "I'm terribly sorry. I didn't catch what you said."

"That's all right. My father was a judge. You must have a very important case, or a very difficult one, if it weighs this heavily on your mind." She smiled in understanding.

"Not really. It's a family thing—that is, clients with family problems."

"And you're caught in the middle," she surmised. "Would you care to discuss it? As much as you can," she added, giving him another understanding smile.

Sloan realized this was an ideal woman for an attorney. Bright. Attractive. Intuitive. Gracious. She would make the perfect mate for an up-and-coming advocate.

However, he didn't much like her perfume. It was too cloying. And her voice was rather high and breathy, as if it was an effort to get the words out.

Husky-throated laughter echoed in his mind, teasing and taunting. By damn, that did it. He was tired of being haunted by Dina Dorelli. "Would you care to stop by my place for a nightcap?" he asked.

Perfectly mascaraed lashes dipped low over lovely blue eyes, then flashed upward in what was supposed to indicate surprise.

With an insight he didn't know he had, he knew she wasn't surprised, that she'd expected the invitation. It annoyed him to be so predictable.

He shoved the irritation aside. He was out with a

charming woman. It was natural to want to continue a pleasant evening, on his part as well as hers. He signaled for the check.

"This is lovely," she murmured when he let them into his place. He'd bought a condo at a good price and was living in it until he found the house he wanted. And the woman he wanted to share it with.

With a start, he realized he was seriously thinking of home and family. Well, it was time. He wasn't getting any younger.

"Did you have professional help?"

He focused on his date. For a moment, he couldn't remember her name. "For what?"

"The decor." She gave him a knowing smile. "Teal blue mixed with earthy tones is something a designer would think of. If you're like my father, you don't know teal from mauve."

"Teal is a mix of blue and green," he informed her. "Mauve is sort of pink. Or purple." Or was it blue? He couldn't remember what his cousin's wife had told him.

Soft, breathy laughter floated over him. He smiled and forced himself to relax. Yes, she would make the ideal companion. Claire. That was her name. Claire.

When she looked up at him, her eyes wide and luminous, it was an invitation, one she knew she was giving, one he knew he was accepting. Good. He liked things open and aboveboard.

He bent to her lips, let his mouth drift across hers. Her lips were moist, already open, inviting him inside...

"I'll put on coffee. Or would you rather have brandy?" he asked, stepping back.

A confused expression ran across her face. She recovered in an instant. "Both, I think. Why don't we start with coffee and switch to brandy later?'' She laid her silk-lined evening cape over the arm of a chair.

Sloan was aware that she trailed after him into the modern kitchen with its granite countertops and white-washed oak cabinets. He made the coffee. His date chatted.

''What did you think of the first half? I thought it was rather slow, but the second act was amusing.''

He suddenly couldn't recall the play they'd seen. Zilch. Nada. God, he was going senile.

''Cats,'' he said, relieved that he'd remembered. And she was... ''Claire.''

She gave him a curious glance.

''Uh, do you take milk or sugar, Claire?'' If a person used a name three times, he was supposed to be able to remember it thereafter. ''Claire,'' he said again to make sure he had it down pat. He did.

''Clarisse,'' she said gently. ''My name is Clarisse. No milk or sugar. I take it as is.''

The blood flushed into his ears. He felt like a kid caught spying through a keyhole. ''Clarisse. Of course. Clarisse,'' he repeated for good measure. Nothing like making a total fool of oneself before a lovely woman. She was being a good sport about it, too.

''Um, this is good,'' she murmured after sipping from the cup he placed before her. ''I didn't realize how cool it could get at night here in the mountains. The day was so warm.''

''Spring is unpredictable up here.'' He took a drink. ''Good grief,'' he said after he managed to swallow. The coffee could have stood on its own. ''I'm sorry. I must have measured wrong. Would you like something else?''

''No, thanks. This tastes like espresso, which I like.'' Her smile was charming.

She was charming. A perfectly charming companion. He'd been swamped with work, taking a briefcase of papers home with him each night and weekends, too. This was a nice break. He was glad he'd let his cousin talk him into taking his wife's visiting friend to the play while they checked on ailing parents.

"Shall we go into the living room?" he asked. He took her by the arm and escorted her to the velvet love seats set at right angles to each other. He flicked a switch and soft lighting lent an intimate atmosphere to the attractive room. "I'll get that brandy, Clar..." He tried to think. He was drawing a blank again. "Clar..."

Her smile never wavered. "Clarisse."

Later, when he'd taken her home and returned to his silent condo, he reflected on the evening. It hadn't been a total failure. In fact, she'd agreed to go to a charity benefit at the opera the following weekend. He was looking forward to it.

Lying in bed, he thought of their good-night kiss. It had been nice...not earthshaking, but nice. He hadn't gotten excited or anything, but that was fine. In fact, that was the way he liked things—cool and calm.

As he drifted into sleep, the memory of another kiss sneaked into his mind. His body sprang to an instant alert. He cursed, then decided to ignore the rambunctious passion that shot through him. Passion did not make for a lasting relationship.

"No," Mr. Dorelli said.

Dina felt the weight of her father's disapproval like a hundred-pound barbell across her shoulders. As a child, she'd been anxious if he so much as frowned, but she was an adult now and she had a job to do.

"We need new equipment," she restated. "The old

won't take the new software.'' She took a deep breath, then added with deadpan calm, ''Don't let your anger with me over marriage mar your business judgment.''

''Watch your mouth,'' Joseph ordered.

She cast him an annoyed glance, then looked back at her father. He had refused to listen to her request for funds to buy a new computer and software package.

For two weeks she had presented him with careful reasoning and the results of her research into the best systems. Her temper had gotten the best of her yesterday. She'd accused him of being stubborn because of her refusal to be engaged. At breakfast, they were still arguing.

''We bought the computer we have five years ago,'' her father reminded her. ''It still works.''

''It's a dinosaur. This new software is flexible. It will handle our orders, balance the checkbook, update the journals and help prepare our taxes. We'll only need one person to take care of all our accounts once it's installed.''

Her father looked shocked. ''Fire Miss Pettibone? She's been with us for forty years.''

''Of course not. We'll need someone to input the data and check the invoices, things like that.'' Dina locked her hands together to keep from waving them around like mad while shouting at her father.

''So what will you do?'' Joseph demanded.

''Check new suppliers for better prices, look for new markets—''

''We deal with our friends, people we've known all our lives,'' her father told her.

''One of those friends cheated us for years.'' She returned his stubborn stare, her silence reminding him that she had been the one who had discovered the fact and exposed it.

He laid a hand on his chest, a troubled expression on his face. The familiar anxiety built in her. She wondered, not for the first time, if he was well. She couldn't imagine a world without him. The emotional distress left from childhood and the death of her mother, a time when her father had been the world, knocked on her heart.

She wasn't a child now, she reminded herself.

She was doing her job...or trying to. As much as her family would let her. With a sigh, she admitted she might never be accepted as a full adult in her family. She was the baby, to be protected and coddled, but not allowed to think for herself. It was a disheartening insight.

An idea that had been taking shape for several days grew stronger. "I resign," she announced.

"What?" Joseph said.

Geoffrey smiled benignly.

Her father sat upright and gave her a piercing glance.

"You don't need me in the business." It was hard to admit. She'd wanted to be needed. "I'll move to Denver and start my own accounting firm." It had sounded so brave and quite simple when she'd thought of it. Now she had only misgivings.

She'd expected the shocked silence. She waited for the anger to erupt. Joseph and her father would talk at the same time, telling her not to be foolish.

The silence drew out...and out...

When she looked at her father, she saw a stillness in his face she'd never seen before. Her own heart chilled.

"You will not leave," he said.

"I must." It was clear now. To have a life of her own, she had to go.

"If you leave this house, I will disown you."

The announcement wrung her heart, almost making her change her mind. She stood.

"Dina, sit down," Geoffrey told her. "We need to discuss this calmly. These Italian tempers," he added with a smile and a shake of his head.

"I don't need a sermon, Geoffrey." She refused to back down from her father's impassive stare.

"If Dina leaves, so will I." Nonna, after sitting quietly during the contretemps, stood, too.

Dina smiled sadly at her grandmother. "I don't know where I'm going. I'll have to find a place, an apartment probably. Or maybe I'll go to the Y."

"Fine," Nonna said. She went to the hall closet and removed her good wool coat and black hat. "I am ready when you are."

Dina sighed and tried to think. Nonna would never be happy away from the land she'd lived on all her adult life. Cut off from her family, she'd wither like a vine without roots.

"I don't have enough money for two people," Dina explained gently. "I'm not sure I have enough for one." Not to mention starting her own business. She glanced once at her father, then left the room quickly before she did something stupid, like cry.

In an hour, she'd packed her compact car to the roof and was ready to leave. Her father had left in the pickup and wasn't there to say goodbye. Her two oldest brothers were, though.

"I'm not going to allow this," Joseph said.

"You can't stop it. I'm almost twenty-five years old." She looked pointedly at her brothers. "Have you ever thought about why we all cluster around here as if we're afraid to venture out into the world—you and Luke in a ranch cottage, Geoff in a parish house two miles from here, Nick in an apartment in town? We're not children. Isn't it time we made our way in the world?''

"You're acting hastily—"

"Please, Geoff, no sermons.'' Dina reached for the door handle, then paused as her grandmother came down the front steps carrying a picnic basket.

"Here's something to take with you.'' She handed the basket over, then cupped Dina's face in her hands. "Be brave,'' she encouraged. "Follow your heart.'' Her smile was one of approval.

Dina nodded and swallowed the lump that rose to her throat. "Tell Nick and Lucien goodbye for me. I'll call you...'' She hugged Nonna fiercely as emotion dried up the words.

"Don't forget to go by the cemetery in Denver.''

"I won't. Bye, Nonna.'' Dina glanced toward her silent, disapproving brothers. She nodded to them and climbed into the loaded car. Heading down the gravel driveway, she had a sudden sense of independence and trepidation.

She was on her own. Uncertainty beckoned like a burning cloud on the horizon as she headed for Denver.

6

Dina scanned the tiny apartment carefully. It was in a nice neighborhood filled with quiet, mostly elderly people. The cemetery was close by. She could check the epitaphs for Nonna.

That almost made her smile.

She returned to the main part of the house. "This is fine."

Her new landlady beamed at her. The landlord smiled and winked ferociously. Since he'd been doing it from the time he answered her knock at the door, she assumed he had a severe tic and wasn't making a pass right in front of his wife.

They discussed the rules of the house. She paid the first and last months' rent, noting the decrease in her bank balance with a gulp. However, she had a goodly sum in her savings account, so she should be all right.

After signing an agreement on her conduct in the house, she returned to her car and began to unpack. Now that she had a place to stay, she felt better. Safer.

By dark, she had her belongings stashed in the three-room apartment. The furniture was dark cherry, antique looking, but the walls were light in the living room and the kitchen, which she suspected had recently been a closet. The appliances were new and apartment-size. Her bedroom was wallpapered in a cheerful wildflower print.

At ten, she took a shower. The bathroom was modern and obviously new. She went to bed after blow-drying her hair.

Looking out the window at the moonlight on the distant mountains, she thought Denver had never seemed so large or the night so dark.

"I think your client should reconsider," Sloan advised his cousin. "The firm's net asset value isn't what they indicated. Our accountant—"

He paused as a commotion in the outer office penetrated the sanctity of the conference room. The noise grew louder.

His secretary's voice came through the heavy walnut door clearly. "You can't go in there. He isn't in his office—"

"Where is he?" an angry masculine voice demanded.

"He's in conference— Wait. You can't— Give me your name and I'll tell—"

The conference room door flew back and bounced off the rubber wall protector. Four burly men walked in.

"I'll get back to you later," Sloan said to his cousin. "This way," he said to the Dorelli brothers. By sheer determination, he managed to shepherd them into the other conference room and close the door. "What is this all about?" he demanded in a stern voice, giving them a fierce scowl to emphasize his authority in the office.

"Dina left—"

"What have you done with her—"

"Did Dina come to you—"

"She refused Tony—"

From this jumbled message, he understood that Dina

had refused the betrothal and had left home. "Calm down," he ordered. He looked at Joseph. "Tell me what happened."

Joseph told the brief story. "Is she at your place?"

"No, she isn't." Something in Sloan's chest grew too big for the space allotted, creating a painful pressure. "You haven't heard from her since...?"

"Since Friday, two weeks ago," the youngest brother confirmed. "She hasn't called Nonna."

The silence that fell on the four brothers attested to their worry about this. Sloan felt it, too. Dina was close to her grandmother. She wouldn't want to worry the elderly lady.

"We thought you might know where she went," one of the middle brothers put in, giving him the suspicious eye.

Sloan studied him. Ah, yes, the preacher who used calm logic to talk another around to his way, according to Dina. Lucien—his brothers called him Luke—was the quiet one. Nick was the youngest and the one closest to Dina.

Sloan picked him to start his questioning. "She didn't tell you where she was going?"

Nick shook his head. "She said she was coming to Denver to start her own business. She and Pop argued about new equipment and some financial package for it."

Sloan suffered a sharp pang of guilt. He was the one who'd told her to assert her authority in the office. It had caused a rift...no, it had been the final straw that broke Dina from her family, it appeared. The refusal of the marriage agreement had been the rift.

"We thought she might have come to you," Nick concluded.

"No, she didn't." Because he'd sided with her father. Because he'd tried to make her see sense. If something happened to her... "I'll hire a private detective."

"Do you know a good one?"

He nodded. "A former police officer. He's the best."

"How much does he charge?"

"I'll take care of it."

Joseph drew himself up. He was close to Sloan's height, but brawnier. "We can pay. You just find her."

"I will," Sloan promised and wondered what they would do if he didn't. Hire a hit man? He gave a derisive snort after the four men—his new clients, he supposed—filed out, leaving behind a ton of advice on how to find Dina and what to do when he did.

"Whew," his secretary murmured when the door closed. "I've never seen so much raw masculinity gathered in one place in my life. Where did they come from?"

"Dorelli Dairy. The four sons."

"They grow them high, wide and handsome down on the farm." She nearly drooled.

"Mary, may I remind you that you're a happily married woman with five grandchildren."

"That doesn't stop me from looking." With a laugh, she returned to her office.

Sloan slumped in his chair and swiveled toward the windows and the view of the mountains that never failed to amaze him.

Dina. That damned little wildcat. Defiant. Headstrong. Spoiled by a doting grandmother and five males who alternately bossed and gave in to her. She *would* be the cause of a split in her family.

He didn't have a clue on how to find her.

His secretary appeared in the doorway between the

offices. "I'm going now. Don't forget—the tickets are in your middle desk drawer. The flowers have been delivered. Have fun." She paused. "Sloan?"

He roused himself from his dark study and forced a smile. "Thanks, I will."

"Is there something else I can do for you?"

"No, you've been a brick."

"You're worried about the Dorelli girl. Surely her family would have heard if anything had happened to her."

The thought of Dina hurt, possibly dead somewhere, went through him like a bolt from a cattle prod. "Yeah, right. I'm going to call Brody on it."

"Brody will find her," Mary assured him. "Well, I'm off. Everyone is gone, and the office is on automatic lock."

He nodded and said good-night. He sat in the sudden quiet for a moment, then called the PI's office. He got the answering machine. Disgruntled, he left his name and hung up. He'd see Brody tomorrow on the handball court at any rate.

The opera droned on like a broken record as far as Sloan was concerned. He was restless. Beside him, Clarisse—he had her name down pat tonight—gave him a smiling perusal with a slight question in her raised eyebrows. He smiled and stared at the stage where the heroine lay dying. He wished she would go ahead instead of singing about it for what seemed like an hour.

He couldn't figure out what was wrong with him. There was a heaviness in his body, the tension of sexual hunger that had been bothering him for weeks.

Glancing at his date, he knew it wasn't coming from

her. Neither was he asleep and dreaming erotic fantasies. He took a deep breath and froze.

That scent. Light. Fragrant as sunlight on a meadow—

The hero came on the stage and sang with the fading heroine. Sloan wished she'd fade faster. He glanced around the rapt audience. Two women were wiping tears from their eyes. A third was moving her lips as if singing along—

By damn, he was going to kill her!

Dina Dorelli sat one row behind and three seats over from him. She obviously knew the Italian words to the melodrama by heart. There were tears in her eyes. Beside her, a man reached into his pocket and offered her his handkerchief.

She took it with a grateful smile and patted her eyes. Sloan wondered if she knew she was with one of Denver's most notorious playboys. His worry for her grew three times bigger.

At last the leading lady expired, the hero wept, everyone was sorry and the drama was over. There was still a backstage party he had to attend. But first—

"Would you excuse me? I'll be right back," he told Clarisse when the audience began to file out. He tried to push his way through the crowd but it was impossible. He'd have to wait until they reached the lobby and there was more room to maneuver.

A husky croak of laughter brought a harsh pang to his nether regions. His libido was at once alert and ready for action.

He muttered an expletive, which earned him a cold stare from the matron in front of him. "Sorry."

She nodded graciously.

Seeing an opening, he went for it, barely squeezing

through before it closed. He was only four people from Dina. Something grabbed his jacket and wouldn't let go.

"Oh," the matron said, annoyed as the lace on her dress pulled into a snag, which was caught on his sleeve button.

"Let me," he said when she fumbled to release them. He pushed the button back through the lace and freed them. When he peered over the matron's head, Dina was nowhere to be seen.

He cursed under his breath.

"Watch your language, young man."

"Watch your damned dress," he retorted, anger rampant. "You made me miss someone I've been looking for."

"If it's a woman, she's wise to avoid you." The matron gave him a disapproving once-over, then proceeded out of the theater.

Sloan made his way back inside. Clarisse waited where he'd left her. A patient woman. He'd have to give more thought to their relationship since she'd decided to remain in Denver now that her divorce was final.

"Did you catch the person you were trying to speak to?" she asked with polite interest.

"No. It wasn't important. A client."

They went backstage where the college players jubilantly hugged one another. He congratulated the director, who was also a friend, on the performance. A gurgle of laughter stopped him cold. Dina.

He searched the crowded backstage area. Her laughter acted as a homing device and he locked in on her. His mouth nearly fell open. She had on the sexiest, most revealing dress he'd ever witnessed.

It was black with straps crisscrossed over the back to well below her waist. When she turned, he breathed a sigh of relief. At least it covered her there, although it was like a second skin, the material so clingy he could tell she wasn't wearing a stitch of underclothes with the outfit.

He did a fast burn. When he got her alone, he was going to give her a talking-to— "What?" he said blankly.

Clarisse nodded toward the leading lady. "Shall we tell her how much we enjoyed the performance?"

He could barely remember there had been a performance. "Uh, sure." He checked on Dina. She seemed intent on staying put, talking gaily with her boyfriend and the hero of the play and sipping freely from a glass of champagne.

After speaking to the star, who was a bright, cheerful graduate student in drama and business, he looked around for Dina again. She wasn't where he'd last seen her.

He searched through the crowd of theater patrons and fans. Dammit. She was nowhere to be seen. If she and that Casanova had left...no, there she was. Ah, heading for the ladies' room.

"Excuse me," he said. He went to waylay her when she came out. Fury churned in him. He'd eat her alive for this little stunt. He took up a position in the dim hall, feeling like Sam Spade hot on the trail of a suspect.

Dina hummed the melody of the heroine's final aria. Such a sad story of love and death and despair. She stepped into the dimly lit hallway and paused, startled, as a large male figure hovered nearby.

"Oh, it's you," she said in relief, recognizing Sloan. "You scared me, skulking around in the dark—"

"I'm much too large for skulking," he informed her.

She tried to decide if he was teasing. He wasn't smiling, so she assumed not. In fact, he looked downright grim.

"The men's room is at the other end of the hall." She put on a bright smile and sternly told her heart to quit jumping around in her chest.

"I don't need the men's room."

"A lecture," she murmured, then sighed and waited for it to be over. "Which of my misdeeds does my father want addressed?"

"This one isn't from your father. It's from me. Why haven't you called your grandmother?"

"Nonna?" Of all the subjects she'd expected him to mention, her grandmother wasn't on the list. She'd talked to her that very morning. "What makes you think I haven't called her?"

"Your brothers came to my office this morning." Sloan gave her a stern frown. "No one has heard from you for two weeks—"

"Excuse me," an annoyed female requested. She squeezed by them in the narrow hall filled with props and went into the ladies' room.

Dina blinked up at him. So, Nonna wasn't telling the hardheaded males of the family where she was or that she'd called. Good. Her life was her own.

"Why haven't you called?"

"It's none of your—"

"Excuse me," the irate female interrupted them again as she left the ladies' room.

Sloan took Dina's hand and tugged her down the hall after the woman to a wider spot.

Dina started over. "It's really none of your business—"

"Pardon me. Is the men's room this way?"

"No," growled Sloan. "It's at the other end."

"Thanks." The man pivoted and ambled off.

Three young women, giggling like mad, entered the hall, heading their way.

Sloan muttered a curse word, shocking Dina. He opened a door tucked between a recliner and a lamp and table. The closet held cleaning supplies on shelves, plus several buckets, brooms and a worn mop. Without a word, he pushed her inside the closet and slammed the door.

"Sloan—"

"Shh."

She was silent until the three passed and went into the bathroom, their laughter cut off as the door closed behind them.

"Ah, peace and quiet," he said in a mocking tone.

"This is ridiculous."

"I agree. I haven't had a moment of peace and quiet since you came up the mountain croaking like a cat with a lethal case of laryngitis."

She graciously ignored the insult to her singing. "It's dark in here. I can't see my hand before my face."

"Your hand isn't before your face," he told her. "There isn't room."

There wasn't. Her chest brushed his with each breath. The toe of his shoe was wedged between hers. When she leaned her head back, she banged it into the shelf behind her.

"Shh," he said again.

"Will you let me out of here?"

"No." He sounded stern again. "Not until I've talked to you. Do you know who you're with this evening?"

She tried to figure out the hidden meaning in the question, but couldn't. "Of course. Baxter Morton—"

"Right. The most notorious playboy in Denver."

"Oh, that. Well, yes, he does have a reputation, but that's because he's on the Denver Broncos. All sports celebrities have reputations—"

"Exactly," Sloan broke in. "No wonder your brothers are worried about you."

She began to see the light, even in the pitch-black closet. "Did my brothers put you up to this?" she demanded, her breasts hitting his chest when she huffed indignantly. She backed off and cracked her skull on the shelf again.

Sloan slid his arm behind her head and rested it on the shelf edge. Her perfume wafted into his nostrils. He leaned closer, wanting another whiff, then caught himself. He was here on a mission. "They came to the office this morning. You've been gone two weeks. I was asked to hire a private investigator to find you."

"For heaven's sake, you'd think I was a lost four-year-old. I'll be twenty-five next week. Isn't that old enough to take care of myself?"

She slipped her hands between them to keep from brushing against him. Her nipples were hard points that ached with delight at each contact. Her insides were going soft and shimmery from his warmth and masculine nearness.

"Yes," he said in a deeper, huskier tone. "But things can happen to a woman alone, no matter how careful she is."

"I'm okay. I have an apartment in the home of an older couple, Mr. and Mrs. Owens, on High Street. They're very nice."

"That should be a relief to your family."

He was intensely aware of her hands lightly resting on his chest, keeping a decent space between them. A restless need rushed over him, making him want to do something crazy and irresponsible...like kiss her until she clung to him instead of resisting him.

Easy, he cautioned. He wasn't here to seduce her. He merely shared her family's concern. She was smart, but inexperienced and ripe for a fall. He didn't want her to land in the lap of someone like the bounder she was with.

He realized he had, at some point, decided to believe that she hadn't known of her father's actions regarding the engagement to her old friend. So maybe she wasn't a lying, two-timing cheat, but she was a sensuous bomb waiting to go off.

He cleared the telltale huskiness from his throat and reached up to brush the sheen of perspiration off his forehead. His hand grazed the side of her breast.

Dina heard the beat of her heart over the quickened shock of their breathing. They stood as if frozen, his hand against her breast, causing a riot of sensation to gather there.

Somehow her hands slid upward to his shoulders. The action lifted her breasts. The pressure of his fingers increased. He drew back. She held her breath. Then his hand closed over her, cupping her breast entirely in his palm. She let the breath out.

"Dina," he said.

A protest, she thought. Then she couldn't think anymore. His arm, the one behind her head, encircled her shoulders. She was hauled against his hard frame.

Her high-heeled pumps gave her extra height. She looped her arms around his shoulders and lifted her head. His chin brushed her forehead, then his lips skimmed along her cheek...down...down and finally reached her mouth.

He mumbled something that sounded like "responsible," but she couldn't hear clearly over the buzz in her head.

The closet, which had seemed much too small, now had loads of room as they wrapped themselves closer and closer until there was no part of her that wasn't snug against him. She moved instinctively against the hard shaft of his desire and heard him groan slightly before sliding a hand down her back to her hips.

He pressed her against him and held her still when she would have moved again. Her head swam dizzily.

"I don't understand," she tried to tell him.

"Yes, you do." His mouth teased at the corners of hers.

Her pulse pounded harder, a drumbeat of hunger in her ears, drowning out all other noise. She leaned into him.

"I've never wanted a woman like this... It's madness..."

She heard some of his words, sensed the angry confusion that caused them, but she couldn't respond. All her senses were concentrated on the wild delight of their caresses.

His hand worked its way between the straps of her dress and curved between her flesh and the built-in bra. She turned, just a bit. His fingers stroked her breast, moved a little, then slid over the tip. He rubbed it again and again.

Desire flared like lightning bolts within her, heating her all the way through. "You were right," she whispered. "I want...I think I want...more."

He groaned and gathered her against him. His lips ravaged hers. She opened to him. He explored her mouth leisurely but thoroughly, then he let her explore his the same way.

The trio of laughing girls erupted into the hallway again. "Where'd that foxy guy go? I want to give him my phone number," one of them declared.

They all laughed again.

"Did you see his eyes?" another asked. "I wish he'd look at me like I was his favorite dessert."

"Yeah, but I think I saw her with Baxter Morton earlier."

"Really? Some people have all the luck."

Their quips pulled Sloan from the brink of disaster. He returned to reality. Realizing where his hand was, he jerked it off her enticing flesh. However, it wasn't easy to get it out of the confounded straps that formed the back of the dress.

"Damnation," he muttered, struggling with the material. "Hold still."

"I'm not moving," Dina said. She slipped her hands into his jacket and caressed him. She found the buttons. It took only a couple of seconds to open them and run her hands over his skin.

"Don't," he warned sternly.

"I know. I shouldn't be doing this. Neither should you." She continued to caress him, liking the tactile sensation of rough hair against her palms. His scent filled her with delight.

"Be still. My watch is caught on your dress."

"That's okay." She snuggled her cheek on his chest, then kissed and tasted him with a shy lick of her tongue. She'd never done that to a man before. He shuddered, and his body jerked against her tummy, telling of his desire.

An enormous feeling of pleasure and satisfaction exploded gently within, spreading a shimmering sensation all over her.

"If this is passion, it's wonderful," she murmured.

"We've got to... We have to think. Stop that." He grabbed at her hands, but she slipped them behind him and caressed his back. She licked his chest again and every inch of her caught on fire as she considered the possibilities.

Sloan tried to turn, his foot kicking a bucket as he did. He froze when he heard voices in the hall. He held the doorknob in case anyone tried to open the closet to investigate the noise.

The women went on by. He released the knob, found the strap caught on his watchband, freed it, then his hand.

Dina kissed all over his chest. With a groan, he sat on the edge of the shelf and hiked her skirt up until he could place her across his thighs. She wore panty hose, he discovered.

Pulling her against him, he savored the lithe perfection of her, all thoughts of caution gone from his mind. Her crooning sounds of delight drove out sense and left only sensation.

He began to move, slowly at first, then faster as she let him guide her into pleasure. At one point, he recognized the voice of her date down the hall. He clasped the doorknob and held her hips with one hand. She had the rhythm now, moving in time with him, the pleasure increasing...

Dina felt the world shrink around her, until there was only her, him...and the wonderful brightness of pleasure between them. It crowded out everything, leaving only the pure brilliance that contracted, then suddenly expanded into a starburst of sensation so strong, she cried out in ecstasy.

Sloan muffled the cry with his mouth, kissing her until she was silent. She rested against him.

Slowly, she became aware of his hand stroking through her hair, smoothing it as he soothed her.

"Sloan," she whispered, unsure of what came next.

"That," he murmured, his lips against her temple, "is what it's all about. Passion. Pure, unreasoning passion."

Taking a deep breath, she raised her head and stared into the dark, unable to see even the outline of his face. Coldness crept around her heart. "Was that a lesson so I'd know what I was missing?"

"No." He stood, made sure she was securely on her feet, then let her go. "That was a mistake on my part. I don't know what happened, but it won't happen again."

She couldn't help it. She giggled.

"I mean it," he said, back in his stern mode. "No more of that. Do you hear me?"

"Yes." She smoothed her skirt. "You'd better button your shirt before we go out."

His hands brushed against her—there was no help for it in the small space—as he made himself respectable. She felt him tuck his shirt in and...arrange things. She wondered how it would be to make love with him completely. In a bed. With all night to explore each other...

She realized he was talking in a low, fierce whisper.

"Do you understand?" he demanded.

"Yes."

He opened the closet door, peered out, then ushered her into the hallway.

"No," she said, realizing she didn't have the foggiest idea what he'd lectured her on.

"Ah, Dina, there you are." Baxter came forward and

took her arm when she and Sloan entered the green room where the party had coalesced as guests began leaving. "Ready to go?"

"Yes. Uh, have you met Sloan Carradine? He's our family attorney. Sloan, this is Baxter Morton. Baxter used to work at the ranch during his high school years. That's how he became such a good runner. He could never remember which field held the breeding bull."

Sloan laughed with the others around them. A tightness between his shoulder blades eased. So Morton was an old friend, another male in the multitude that made up Dina's life. Did she think of him as a brother the way she did Tony?

Meeting Baxter's watchful, yet rueful gaze, he thought she probably did. Pride filled him with a pleasant buzz. At least she knew *he* was a man. She'd responded to him as a woman, not a sister, each time they'd touched.

And she now knew what real pleasure was between a man and a woman— Hold it. Just hold on there.

He'd lectured her about lust and true feelings of love between a man and a woman while they were rejoining the party. They shared a great passion, but nothing else. A long friendship was the basis of a long relationship. He didn't even know her favorite color.

"Nice to have met you," Baxter said, taking Dina's hand and tucking it in the crook of his arm. "You should wipe the lipstick off before you rejoin your date," he suggested before walking off with Dina.

Her laughter remained behind like the dying gurgle of a strangled horse. Sloan swiped at his mouth, feeling dangerously close to strangling something himself, and looked around for Clarisse. Now there was a woman who knew what was what. He set his jaw and went to find her.

7

Dina surveyed her office with satisfaction. She was now the junior partner in a two-man, uh, two-person firm. By checking out the local businesses, she'd found an accountant who was overworked and needed help. Tom Mix—no kin to the actor—had read over her credentials and accepted her on the spot.

So she was all set—a job, an apartment, a life.

After placing a row of herbs and ivy on the windowsill, she hung her diplomas and certification on the wall. She was filled with pride as she took in her new desk, credenza and bookcases. Her books were in place, and she was ready for business. Or would be when the office opened on Monday.

Sitting in her executive chair, she peered at the trees that lined the freeway. Some view.

She swallowed hard as emotion collected like a solid lump of clay in her chest. Today was her birthday.

A knock on the front office door roused her before she sank too deeply into self-pity. She'd get used to life in the city. She'd better. She intended to stay.

Going to the door, she peered out and started in surprise. Sloan. She released the dead bolt and opened the door. "Hi. Are you lost or slumming?" she asked with fake cheer.

Her heart thumped like a jackhammer. For eight nights, she'd dreamed of those kisses and caresses they'd exchanged in the closet... A *closet*, for heaven's sake.

Sloan's eyes raked over her, then settled on her name plaque beside the door. He ignored her inquiry. "Looks like you're in business."

"Yes." She couldn't believe how handsome he looked. Today he was in jeans, sneakers and a polo shirt. His hair was damp, as if he'd recently showered. She resisted the urge to touch it.

"Your brothers asked me to check that you were okay. You still haven't called them." He gave her a stern frown.

"I told Nonna she could tell them I'd called. How did you find me?"

"I looked up Owens on High Street in the telephone book. When I stopped by the house, some man told me you lived there and that you were at your new office. He kept winking at me. I wasn't sure if he was joking or not."

Dina laughed. "Yes, that was my landlord. I thought he was making a pass when I first went there, but since his wife was present, I decided he had a tic. She told me later he'd had a minor stroke last year that had affected one side of his face."

Sloan's frown softened in sympathy. A long silence ensued. He shifted restlessly, a tall, big-boned man with the gentlest touch. He stuck his hands in his pockets.

With something akin to despair, she admitted she wanted him to touch her again. She wanted his hands all over her—

"Have you had lunch?" he asked abruptly.

She checked her watch in surprise. "It's almost one.

I didn't realize the morning had gone. Come admire my office,'' she invited on an impulse.

Her lips tingled as she led the way into her inner sanctum. She was aware that it was Saturday, and no one was there but her and Sloan. However, the shopping center was busy with customers buying groceries or auto parts or ice cream.

''Very nice,'' he said, leaning against the doorframe. ''The plants are a friendly touch. I'm adding a ficus to my office after seeing the one in yours at the dairy.''

''The view isn't as great here,'' she told him, chatting to hide the nervousness he caused.

He glanced out the window and back at her. ''You miss the mountains.''

The view from the dairy office appeared in her mental vision. She nodded. ''I suppose.''

''And your family,'' he surmised. ''I called your brothers.''

Her head came up. ''Did you tell them where I was?''

He nodded.

''You rat.''

His smile was coolly amused. ''I thought it best, for your sake as well as theirs. They were worried. One or more called me every day to find out if the private investigator had found out where you were.''

''You knew I was okay. Are you getting a kickback from the detective to refer cases to him?''

He gave her a pained look. ''Hardly. I didn't put him on the case. As you said, I knew where you were. I wasn't sure about the okay part.''

''Why?''

''Baxter Morton. Joseph didn't like it when he heard you were with the sports star.''

''Joseph is a mother hen. I was a scrawny kid in

braces when Baxter worked at the ranch. He treated me like a sister.''

"He didn't look at you as if you were a sister Friday night," Sloan reminded her. "I wouldn't have let my sister out of the house in the dress you were wearing."

"Yeah, and she'd have left home as I've had to do in order to have a life of my own."

"Running around with celebrity jocks? Is that your idea of a life? Are you going to become a groupie?"

Dina was taken aback at the harshness in Sloan's voice. Gone was the earlier coolness. He was definitely hot under the collar. Like her family, he seemed to think she had no judgment at all.

"Baxter was a perfect gentleman," she informed him. "That's a lot more than I can say about you."

His scowl became darker, more deadly. He stalked toward her. She retreated behind her desk, a position of authority.

"Is that right?" he demanded.

A frisson breezed up her arms and into her scalp. "Yes. I wonder what my brothers would say if they knew about you forcing me into that closet, then accosting me—"

"Accosting?" he repeated, his dark tawny eyebrows lifting in amusement. "Who wore a dress so sexy she had men falling over their tongues when she sashayed by?"

She had no defense. The dress had been a recent purchase, part of her new image, that of a woman, not a kid sister. Maybe she'd overdone it a bit. Even Baxter had asked if she meant what the dress had implied.

"Whose laughter sounds like an invitation to pure, unadulterated sex?" Sloan continued relentlessly.

"Mine?" Her voice squeaked upward, broke, then dropped to husky surprise, all on one word.

He leaned over the desk and pointed a finger. "Yours. Who can blame a man for losing his head—" He stopped abruptly, then dropped his hand and retreated to the door.

She was disappointed. She wanted to hear more about her irresistible allure. No one had ever mentioned it, not like Sloan did, as if it were a foregone fact.

"Do you want lunch or not?" he asked, sounding as if he would rather wrestle a warthog.

"Yes." She snatched up her purse, locked her desk and indicated she was ready to go.

They left without speaking. He escorted her to a tiny restaurant tucked into the corner of the shopping center. It was busy, but quiet, its interior an atrium of hanging plants.

"How lovely," she commented, surprised.

"I thought you'd like it." He returned to the menu.

"You've been here before?" She was instantly jealous.

"Yes. It isn't that far from the office. My secretary chose it for her birthday lunch."

"Oh." So he hadn't brought the gorgeous woman he'd been with at the opera. She ordered a grilled chicken salad when the waitress returned. Sloan ordered the same.

When they were alone, she rubbed a finger over the icy haze on the water glass. Without looking at her companion, she asked, "Who was your friend the other night? Is she your steady date?"

"Clarisse? My cousin's wife recently introduced us. No, she isn't what you'd call a steady, although I'm not seeing anyone else." He thought this over, then smiled.

"Unless one counts a certain minx who's driving me crazy. Not to mention her four brothers."

"You're not dating me."

He lifted his wineglass. "We're having lunch."

She lifted her water glass. "My birthday luncheon."

"Today is your birthday?"

She nodded. At home, Nonna and Lupe would have prepared her favorite dishes for dinner. There would have been a huge cake and tons of presents. All the family would have been there.

"You must feel lonely." An emotion flickered through those sky blue eyes. Pity?

"Not at all," she quickly denied. "I'm not a child. After twenty-five years, birthdays aren't a big event."

"A quarter century, and she hasn't lost her hair or teeth yet. Will wonders never cease?"

His teasing confused her, making her go soft inside and filling her with longing. She realized this was the best birthday present—a surprise lunch with a handsome man.

During the meal, she told him about her business partner and his wife, who worked as their receptionist-secretary. It wasn't until they left the restaurant that she realized he'd skillfully drawn her out until he knew as much as she did.

"I'll walk you to your car," he offered.

"I walked down. It's only three blocks."

"Then I'll walk you home."

"Why?"

"It's a beautiful day. You're a beautiful woman. What could be better?"

Flowers were in bloom everywhere. Tulips and buttercups, forsythia, hawthorn bushes. The sky was as shiny as porcelain. The trip didn't take near long enough.

He went up with her to look at her apartment. He smiled at the pots of jonquils blooming by the window. "Very nice."

"Would you like some coffee?"

He hesitated, then shook his head. "I'll let your family know that all is well with your living and working arrangements."

"Then you'll be finished with me?" Her smiling glance was a deliberate challenge. She wanted to put him on the spot and see how he would handle it.

Again he hesitated. "Yes. There will be no need for us to meet again. Unless for business reasons, of course. I hope you'll remember our firm if you need legal advice."

"And I hope you'll remember mine if you need financial advice." She kept her tone as cool and impersonal as his.

He opened the door to the stair landing. "Goodbye, Dina."

"Goodbye. Thanks for lunch."

When he left, she went to the window and watched him walk back the way they had come. The apartment surrounded her in silence. A sense of loneliness caught up with her all of a sudden. She blinked until the strange emotion passed, then started on her housework.

At four, five baskets of flowers arrived. By five, there were two more plus three boxes of candy. She cried as she read the cards from her family and Tony, all wishing her well and telling her to come home soon.

She couldn't. More and more, she was coming to view her move as the right one. It was time she made her own way in the world and found a place for herself away from her family's influence and protection. But she missed them.

* * *

After the movie, Clarisse invited Sloan to her apartment. She was settled in and was enthusiastic about her new job. He briefly wondered how Dina was liking her independence.

He scowled. Dina Dorelli was not his responsibility.

"Why so solemn?" Clarisse asked. She placed coffee and dessert on the marble table in front of the sofa. Her place reminded him of his condo—modern, in good taste, dull.

"Sorry. I don't mean to be poor company."

"You're not." Her smile showed she meant it.

She was a lovely person, not pushy, not argumentative, but not a wimp, either...a lady in the best meaning of the term.

After they had the apple pie, which she'd baked, she cleared the dishes, then settled beside him on the love seat. Her gaze was seductive...and determined.

He knew danger in a situation when he saw it. He rose abruptly. "Ah, the bathroom?"

The startled expression disappeared. She smiled languidly and stretched like a cat. "Down the hall. On your right."

He hightailed it out of the living room. The only problem, he acknowledged, was he had to go back. After a longer-than-necessary sojourn, he ventured into the living room.

"Well, I guess I'd better be going," he said with just the right amount of regret underlining the words.

"It's not even eleven. Come, sit." She patted the seat beside her. "I've poured fresh coffee."

He sat. After taking a sip of the coffee, he glanced at the darkness outside the window. "I can't stay long," he said.

"You don't have court tomorrow," she reminded him with a low murmur of laughter.

He remembered laughter that started out on one octave, then dropped to a lower one as it gurgled into silence like a dying gasp. An involuntary smile sprang to his lips.

"Share?" Clarisse invited.

"Uh, it was nothing...a client," he added when she gave him a disbelieving glance.

She leaned into him with a lazy glide that took him by surprise. Her lashes dropped to the halfway mark. "I won't break if you kiss me," she said playfully.

He'd hardly done more than brush across her mouth when they said good-night after their dates. He'd been seeing her once, sometimes twice, a week for a month.

They'd had dinner at his cousin's home twice. His cousin's wife saw them as a couple. His cousin had asked how things were coming along between them the other day at the office. As Clarisse moved seductively against him, her actions made it clear she was ready to move to a more intimate level.

Looking at the invitation in her smile, he realized he didn't know what her expectations were but knew he didn't want to casually drift into an intimate relationship. For some reason, the idea repelled him.

"Excuse me," he said. He yanked out his handkerchief and faked a sneeze. "Sorry. Must be catching a cold."

"That's okay. I'll take extra vitamin C."

She was so damned agreeable, it grated on his nerves. He sneezed a couple more times. "I'd better go." He gave her a buss on the forehead and leapt from the sofa before she could do more than blink.

An irritated frown appeared on her face before she

slipped into her usual smile and followed him to the door. Sloan felt as if he was being stalked.

"Come to dinner tomorrow night," she invited.

"Uh, I think I'd better stay home and nurse this cold."

"Next week, then."

"I already have plans." He did. He decided then and there to go to his cabin and spend some time alone. Women and their damned machinations were driving him right off the deep end.

At once she looked suspicious. "Are you—" She paused and took a moment to choose her words. "I'm not seeing anyone else. I had assumed you weren't, either."

"I do have other friends," he told her gently but firmly, rejecting the load of guilt she pushed his way.

"Of course." She smiled bravely. "I may go visit my folks in Arizona. I haven't seen them for a while."

There was a subtle threat in her statement. She might meet someone else. She might not come back. She might look for someone more interesting.

"Shall I drive you to the airport?" he asked.

"No. I'll take a cab." Her tone was cool.

He headed for the door and was soon on his way. Driving home, he argued with his conscience. Dammit, he hadn't done anything wrong. He hadn't led her on or made any promises. It wasn't as if he'd ever lost his head and kissed her like mad and caressed her as if there was no tomorrow—

An image of a woman he had done all those things to erupted in his mind. His body, which hadn't reacted earlier, now came to hard, painful life. He cursed, words he didn't even know he knew, the rest of the way to his condo.

* * *

Dina locked the office behind her. She'd worked late every night that week. Although it was the middle of May, many of her clients were late with their taxes. She'd filed extensions for them and was up to her ears in work. It was a new experience. Keeping books at the dairy had been duck soup compared to this.

"Oh." She jerked as a tall male appeared by her side. "Luke, you scared me."

"Beware the jabberwocky," he told her in his usual laconic style.

"Translation—watch out for muggers and such when you step out of the office?"

"Something like that. Brother Joe says it so much better than I do."

"And goes on saying it until I want to scream." She squeezed his arm. "I'm so glad to see you. It seems ages since I've seen anyone from home."

"Someone calls every day."

"Well, Joseph does. Or Tony, sometimes. He just chats, though, instead of lecturing. So does Nick. Geoffrey sermonizes about the sins of the city and a country-bred girl like me falling into them, but that's his calling."

Lucien chuckled. "Joseph tried to assign us days to call, but no one would go along."

She rolled her eyes. "Thank heavens. Have you had dinner? I'm starved."

"Me, too. I was hoping you'd invite me."

"Sure. I'm a businesswoman now. Make all kinds of money."

Laughing, they went to her favorite restaurant at the shopping center. It wasn't until Luke dropped her at her place at ten that she felt the full impact of loneliness again. She sank down on the sofa and contemplated the feeling.

Her life had been full and happy six weeks ago. Then her father had gotten stoked up about her getting married. She wished Tony hadn't been for it, too. It had changed her relationship with him and with her family.

Why did he have to fall in love with her? Why hadn't she fallen in love with him?

A picture of Sloan slipped into her mind.

She wasn't in love with *him*. She hardly knew him. For some strange reason, they both went wild when they touched, but that wasn't love. She was sure of it. So was he.

Of course, her parents had fallen in love immediately, and they couldn't have known much about each other. It was difficult to think of her father as an impetuous, passion-driven young man. It was equally hard to think of Sloan that way. And he wasn't, not really. Except when they kissed.

She sighed, but couldn't figure out what it all meant. At any rate, it had been wonderful to see Luke tonight and hear all his news on the family. She did miss them, even though she and Nonna did talk every day.

Dina hurried into the post office. She'd made it right before closing. She dropped a stack of letters in the slot, then turned to head back for the office. She would be working late tonight. As usual.

Rushing to the door, she opened it, then held it politely for the next person to enter. She gazed into eyes as blue as the sky. "You just made it," she said with false gaiety. "They close in five minutes."

"I wasn't coming to the post office. I saw you from my car and decided to stop." His gaze drifted over her with a moody thoroughness. "You want to have dinner?"

"I'm tempted," she admitted, "but I have a stack of tax forms waiting at the office I need to get done tonight."

"You're keeping long hours."

"This is the busy season."

There was an awkward pause. Dina moved aside when a woman dashed up to the door. Sloan took her arm and guided her outside to the shade of a sycamore tree. "Are you all right?"

She realized he sounded like one of her brothers, checking up on her state of health. Where once she would have answered with a smart remark, now she spoke seriously. "Yes. Really. I love my work. My life is…interesting and busy."

"Good." He heaved a deep breath. "No, it isn't. I want you to be as miserable as I am. Isn't that a laugh?"

Currents ran between them, strong ones, like a river filled with spring wash, rushing madly to a destiny it didn't know or care about. There was only the moment and the wild flow.

"No. I don't think it's funny." She looked up at him. "Don't stop for me again, Sloan. I'd rather you didn't. My life is easier when you don't. I can handle the wanting better if you're not around."

He opened his mouth, closed it, then finally spoke. "I see. That was a very honest statement."

"Coming from a woman."

"I didn't say that."

"But you thought it." She hesitated. "I don't know much about your experiences with women, but there's a distrust in you that doesn't bode well for your future happiness if you ever find someone to marry. Try to get over it,'' she advised.

He smiled slightly. "I'm the one who's supposed to dispense advice. I get paid for it."

"Consider it a gift." She looked at her watch. "I've got to go. Have a nice evening." She hurried down the steps and to her car. The traffic was heavy, and she had no time to dwell on their conversation on the way back to the office.

It was just as well. She had her work to think about. But, she reflected as she parked in her usual spot, Sloan had sounded almost sad...and sort of caring, too. She wasn't going to dwell on that, either.

The telephone was ringing when she let herself back in the office. She dashed across the room and picked up. "Hello?"

"Dina?" Joseph said.

"Yes, Joseph."

He went through his list of reasons why she should stop this nonsense and return home.

Dina rubbed her eyes, which were tired from looking at receipts and numbers all day. "I'm not coming back. I have a life here, one I enjoy," she said firmly. They'd gone over this several times of late.

"You're just being stubborn."

"I suppose." She was also weary.

"You belong here. With Tony."

"Leave Tony out of this. He understands. You're just mad because I won't do what you want me to. You're not my boss. Nobody died and left you in charge of the world, Joseph. You should relax and take care of your cows."

There was a long pause on the phone line. Her partner

waved good-night to her from the open door to her office. She smiled and waved back.

"I'll talk to you tomorrow about the Tomlin case," he said.

"Okay."

"Who was that?" her brother asked.

"No one." She looked back at the papers on her desk. She wanted to finish them tonight. "I have to go."

"Is there a man with you?" Joseph demanded. "Are you seeing someone?"

"I wish," she mumbled...and thought of Sloan and his strange visit. An idea came to her...

"Dina, watch yourself," he warned sternly. Since their mother had died he'd changed from a laughing daredevil to a serious-minded curmudgeon who seemed to think he was responsible for everyone's health and welfare. She was really too tired to indulge his need to boss everyone in sight.

"It may be too late. I've met someone—"

"Who? What's his name?"

"He's just a man." She spoke hesitantly, as if the words were torn out of her against her will. She was making them up as she went along. "He's older... and...he's very exciting, a man unlike any I've ever known, sophisticated but with a quiet reserve that thrills me. I never know what he's thinking."

Joseph nearly broke her eardrum with his roar. "Don't you let him touch you. Do you hear? He's just... Men don't... I'm telling you, Dina, don't fall for any line, hear?"

She changed the phone to the other ear. "Yes, Joseph. You're right. I'll not see him again. I'll hang up when he calls and begs me to come over to his place—"

"*What!*"

She was beginning to enjoy the story. Ignoring the jab of her conscience, she elaborated more. "It's just that there's this irresistible passion between us—"

"Who is he? Tell me right now!"

"I can't. You mustn't hurt him. I couldn't bear it. He's so handsome, like a Greek statue, only better looking. His nose isn't broken off." She smiled at the inane quip as longing and fatigue rolled over her. There would be no Greek gods in her future, not after she'd told Sloan to stay out of her life.

"I'll break his damned nose if he's touched you," Joseph promised darkly, quieter now.

Dina worried briefly about that quiet tone. However, her brother couldn't hurt someone who didn't exist. "Well, he hasn't. Things haven't progressed...hmm, too far. Oh, I have to go. Someone's at the door. It might be him."

She waited out her brother's lecture not to lose her head, not to believe the bastard and to come home immediately.

"Not for love nor money," she declared, replacing the phone when the one-sided conversation finally ended.

She liked her life fine. It was a bit lonely at times, but she was doing well, making more money than she ever had. She was adding to her savings account weekly. Because she rarely had time to spend a cent due to the workload.

She started adding a column of figures again. A half hour later, the phone rang. It was Geoffrey.

"How are you, baby face?" he said, using an old nickname for her. "What's this Joe tells me about some older man you've met?"

With a grimace of irritation, she began her absurd

story for the second time. "Oh, he's wonderful, so mature, so handsome, so charming." She paused to see how Geoff would take this syrupy eulogy before she poured more on. He surely wouldn't fall for her fabrication.

"Dina," he said hesitantly. He was nothing if not diplomatic. "You're young—

"Twenty-five. Did you get my thank-you note for the flowers? That was so thoughtful."

"Yes." A bit impatiently. "Flattery is like a flower, easy to hand out, but not lasting. Friendship is a rare gem, to be treasured for a lifetime."

"You're absolutely right."

"Well...yes. About this man, an older one, you said?"

"Somewhat. In his thirties, at least."

"At least?"

Dina heard the surprise. She had him going now. She wondered what she'd ever done to make her brothers think she was a pushover for a smooth line. Having grown up with them, she certainly understood the basic instincts of the male of the species. "He might be closer to forty. He's reserved and rather quiet."

Except when they touched. That had been so wild and sweet and shattering, even the memory was devastating.

"...I'll talk to you later," Geoff was saying sternly. "Don't do anything you'll regret. Remember the parable of the wise virgins and the foolish ones."

The foolish virgins had fallen asleep and missed the wedding feast, if she remembered correctly. The wise ones had kept their lamps trimmed and been watchful. They could have woken the others up, she'd always thought. "Yes. I'm certainly burning the midnight oil. All this work. I won't fall asleep, I assure you," she said cheerfully.

He talked another ten minutes in his calm, reasonable manner. She agreed with every homily he threw at her. Finally, he ran out of them and said goodbye.

Twenty minutes later, the phone rang again.

She debated whether to answer. On the fifth ring, she picked up. "Hello?"

"Dina, it's Tony."

"Tony," she said warmly. "How are you?"

"Fine."

"Thank you for the candy. That was sweet. You remembered my favorite chocolates."

"Yeah, right. Listen, Joe thinks you're involved with some man down there in Denver. Geoff does, too. In fact, they think they know who it is."

His ominous pause sent goose bumps over her scalp.

"Who?" she asked on a croaky breath.

"Sloan Carradine."

Her heart stopped beating. "Sloan? How silly." Her laugh didn't quite come off.

"We're going into town tomorrow and see him at his office as soon as it closes."

"We?"

"I thought I'd tag along."

"Is Nick in on this?"

"'Fraid so."

"He's an officer of the law. They could take his badge away if there's trouble. He loves being a cop."

"Yes, but this is a family matter. I'll bail them out of jail if it gets down to that."

She recalled Sloan's insouciance on the dance floor when she'd warned him what her brothers would do if he held her too close. "If there's a fight, Sloan won't back down."

"Do you want me to tell your father?"

"No. I'm already in trouble with him. If he knew the fibs I've told—"

"So you're not involved with an older man?" There was relief in his voice. He was as concerned for her well-being as her brothers, but he didn't try to tell her what to do. She loved him for that alone.

"Of course not. But, Tony, I am attracted to Sloan," she felt honor-bound to add.

"I understand."

She knew he did. The affection she'd always felt for him filled her, but it wasn't love, not the kind she'd dreamed of. It wasn't enough for marriage. She didn't know how she knew that but she did. He was her best, her oldest, friend, but she would never marry him.

Closing her eyes, she fought a sudden need to weep. This wasn't the time for tears. "Try to stop my crazy brothers. I'll tell Sloan to get out of his office and hide until they come to their senses."

"Will do. Take care, pug." It was his name for her from childhood days, referring to her short, upturned nose. She'd fought him over it. A lump formed in her throat. She wished she were a child again, with all the delight of those days and none of the worry of these.

"I will. Tony…" She didn't know what to say.

He laughed, a wry note in it. Maybe sadness, too. "Yeah, I know. You love me like a brother."

"I love you more than my brothers, except maybe Nick."

"Ever honest," he murmured, again with the wry undertone. "I love you, too, kid, but that's another story. I'll let you know what develops on the home front."

"Please do."

After they said goodbye, she looked in the phone book for Sloan's number. It wasn't listed. She muttered one of her brothers' favorite curse words. She'd go to his office tomorrow and try to save his life...well, his nose, at any rate.

8

⟶⟵

Dina was glad she'd called Sloan's office first thing that morning. She'd asked when his last appointment was and had been told his schedule was filled that morning. He would be out of the office for the afternoon. She'd been relieved.

Until Tony had called and told her that her brothers had also checked on Sloan and now intended to be there at noon when he left the office.

She checked her watch. Eleven. She called Sloan's office again. The secretary reported he was with a client.

"Please have him call me as soon as he's free. It's..." Well, it wasn't a matter of life or death. "It's important," she finished, trying to sound firm and hoping she didn't come across as a hysterical female.

"I'll tell him." The secretary was decidedly cool.

Staring at the trees alongside the freeway, Dina considered. Really, she had no obligation to Sloan. She should stay out of it and let the men handle the situation. Ten-to-one odds they'd all end up at a bar, laughing about the misunderstanding and guzzling beer by five. Men were such Neanderthals.

She checked the time. Eleven-fifteen.

Sloan would be okay. Her brothers wouldn't jump him all at once. They did have a code of honor. They'd draw straws to see who got to beat him up. Maybe he would be gone before they arrived at his office.

If not, he would explain to them that he wasn't the man she had referred to in her older-man scenario. Unless her brother, whichever won the right to fight him, hit first and asked questions later.

Did Sloan know how to fight? He came from back East. They probably had rules. He wouldn't know about the no-holds-barred brawls out here.

Why should she worry about him? Of course, she had told those tall tales to her brothers... But was it her fault they jumped to the wrong conclusions?

Hardly.

She bit at a ragged cuticle, making it worse. She looked at her watch. Eleven thirty-five.

The waiting was murder...don't use that word.

Finally, she made a decision. After sliding her work into a briefcase, she went to her car. At her apartment, she stuffed a nightshirt and a change of clothes into an overnight case.

As she was leaving she saw the light on her answering machine blink. It was from Tony. He'd warned her she'd better get to Sloan's, else there might be bloodshed, because Joseph had drawn the shortest straw.

He was the most formidable brawler of the bunch. Dina thanked her landlord, then set out at a run for her car. She reached the elegant building that housed Sloan's office without getting stopped by a cop and parked in the loading zone.

She had to check the directory, wasting precious time, to get the suite number. The elevator took forever to get to the seventh floor. As soon as the door opened a handspan, she lunged through. And nearly ran over Sloan.

He looked as surprised as she was.

"Sloan! Thank heavens." She glanced around. No one else in sight. She kept one hand on the elevator door. "We've got to get you out of town."

"I'm leaving now," he informed her, his smile quizzical, his tone sardonic.

Another elevator opened. She peered anxiously into it. No one was there. The hair stood up on the back of her neck. She glanced up and down the long hallway.

"Are we looking for anyone in particular?" Sloan inquired.

"My brothers. Believe me, you don't want to see them."

"What's happening?"

She took his arm and pulled him into the elevator. On the way down, she told him about her brothers coming to beat him up. She peered at him from under her lashes to see how he took this news. He appeared equally amused and mystified.

"Why would they do that?"

"They, uh, sometimes get a bee in their collective bonnets. It's...well...I'll explain it all later. We've got to get you out of town until things cool down and I can talk to them."

"Where are we going?"

"To your ranch. You can hide out there—"

"Dina, I am not going to hide out," he said firmly, stopping them in the middle of the sidewalk.

She saw a pickup truck with red pinstriping at the corner. Joseph. He'd have to circle the block because of the one-way street, though. They could still get away.

"Hurry." She tugged Sloan to her car and pushed him inside. She took off with a screech of tires.

"A life on the run," he mused. "I always wondered if it would be fun. It certainly is shaping up that way.

We can be a modern Bonnie and Clyde.'' He ogled her in a lecherous fashion.

"This isn't a joke." She turned the corner, made the next green light by a whisker, cut in front of three cars turning left on a green arrow onto the freeway and headed west.

"I believe the speed limit is still fifty-five in town," Sloan mentioned in conversational tones.

She cast him an annoyed frown and lifted her foot a quarter inch. They drove in silence until the traffic thinned. She speeded up as they climbed into the mountains, then slowed for the exit to the country road that led to his home and hers forty minutes later. Her former home, she corrected.

Soon they arrived at the gravel driveway to his place. She drove carefully over the deep ruts caused by winter rains. Tension coiled in her as they neared the house.

"Ah, I've missed this place," he murmured. After rolling down his window, he breathed deeply and watched the scenery slip by. "I have cows on my land now, about fifty of them. The rancher next door and I are partners in a small herd."

"Good. That will give the herd some new grazing." She stopped in front of his house.

"Come on in," he said. "I'm hungry. Next time you kidnap me at lunch, I'll expect you to bring food."

"Yeah, right." She looked at his cabin and remembered all the things that had happened during her sojourn there once before. "I'd better get on home...to Nonna's."

"And leave me stranded here all weekend?"

"Oh. I hadn't thought about that." Something else came to mind. "You didn't...you weren't seeing your, uh, lady friend this weekend, were you?"

"No. I don't think she's my friend anymore. We had a slight disagreement."

Gladness surged through her. She bit the inside of her lip until the smile went away. "I'm sorry."

"Why? It wasn't your fault." He paused. "Or maybe it was." He laughed.

Startled, she stared at him.

He explained. "If I hadn't wanted to kiss you so much, maybe I would have wanted to kiss her more."

"Did you kiss her?" She winced. She couldn't believe she'd asked so dumb a question.

"A peck, nothing more." He eased his tall frame out of her compact car. "Lunch?" he invited.

She fiddled with the keychain. "You can drive me home and keep my car until Sunday—"

"You're the one who kidnapped me," he broke in, a challenge in his eyes. "You have to entertain me for the weekend." In a few long strides, he was at her side, holding the door open and waiting for her to get out.

Her pulse leapt. She'd been intensely aware of him on the journey, although she'd tried not to. He had filled the space between them with his presence. "Is that wise?"

Sloan was taken by the candor of the question and in her eyes. He liked it that she admitted the attraction. In his experience, most women weren't that honest about the physical side of things. "I may be able to control myself."

"I might not." She smiled ruefully and climbed out.

He saw the cases in the back seat and retrieved them. Inside, he took them to her bedroom, then set about finding something for lunch. Fortunately, the refrigerator had a large freezer section that he'd stocked the last time he was there.

Soon he had sandwiches and chips on the table. He opened a couple of windows. ''Madam?'' He held a chair for her.

''I can't believe it's almost June,'' she mused as she ate. ''This is the best time in the mountains. Warm days, cold nights. Wildflowers everywhere and snow still under the pines.''

''Yes, it's beautiful.'' He was looking at her instead of the scene outside. He realized she really was beautiful in a natural kind of way. He fought the urge to touch her.

He had a hard time when her tongue flicked over her lips and caught a crumb. He was playing with fire and he knew it. He shouldn't have acceded to her kidnapping scheme, but since he'd planned to come here anyway, it had been amusing to go along with her plan.

Who was he kidding?

He'd come because he wanted to be alone with her at the cabin. He wanted to do things to her that would probably shock her inexperienced little socks off.

''Two months,'' he said, watching her chew and swallow, then take a drink of cola.

''Not quite.''

He smiled as she caught on immediately to what he was thinking. It meant her mind was running in the same track.

''I've thought of you every single day...and night.'' He shook his head in wonder at this confession. ''What are we going to do about it?''

A pretty shade of pink highlighted her cheeks. ''Sounds like a personal problem to me.''

The attempt at nonchalance was spoiled by the slight tremor in her hand when she lifted the sandwich again. An odd sense of tenderness mingled with the lust he felt for her. He finished his meal, then reached over and ran a fingertip along her warm cheek. "I think not."

She shrugged and moved away from his touch, but he'd seen the sharp catch of her breath and the slow, careful release that exposed her awareness of the thing between them.

Elation rose in him. He didn't stop to question it. Leaning back in the chair, he relaxed. "We have all weekend," he said, realizing it was true.

He doubted her brothers would come looking for him. His secretary had been instructed to tell anyone who inquired that he was out of town on a case. He hadn't thought it would be Dina's family, but that was okay.

"For what?" Her voice broke and dropped to a sexy level.

"To have fun." He stood, aware of the desire surging through his veins. For the first time in months, he felt totally alive and in tune with nature. "Come on, finish up. We're going to fish for our supper. Can you cook trout?"

"Of course."

He tousled her hair. "Of course. With Nonna for a grandmother, you'd have to, wouldn't you?"

Her croaky laughter rang out. "She moved in with us after my grandfather died and was scandalized that an eleven-year-old couldn't make anything but brownies."

They changed clothes and climbed down to the creek at the base of the cliff. There, under an alder tree, was a pool where trout were sure to lurk. He fixed a line for her. "You know how to fly-fish?"

Dina gave him a disgusted grimace. Taking the pole, she whipped it over their heads, playing out line, then popped the fly into the shadow of the overhang on the opposite bank.

On her third cast, she got him.

"A rainbow," he shouted. "Bring him in. Keep the line tight. Pull up. Reel. That's it. That's it. Come to papa, beauty," he crooned as he grabbed the fish. "Ah, a gorgeous little female. Go home, darling, and raise a bunch more just as beautiful as you."

She studied him while he released the fish back into the cold, clean water. "How come guys can say all kinds of sappy things to a fish, but not to a woman?"

"Fish don't laugh at 'em."

"I don't laugh at men."

One tawny eyebrow rose fractionally. "No? But you tell stories. I want to hear the one that decided your brothers to come after me."

Her ears grew hot. "I told them I was involved with an older man."

"You told them you were having an affair with me?" He looked ready to throttle her.

"No, no. I just said someone older, very handsome and, um, rather quiet and reserved. They were the ones who jumped to the conclusion it was you." She gave him her most innocent look. "I was making up the story as I went. I figured they couldn't hurt someone who didn't exist."

"Huh," he snorted.

"I wasn't talking about you. I never thought... It was just that they kept giving me advice—for my own good, of course—so I gave them something else to think about," she defended her actions. "I thought they'd quit telling me to come home and marry Tony if they thought there was someone else."

He moved in closer, his eyes narrowed.

"I didn't think they'd think it was you."

"Who the hell else would they think of?" he demanded. "I'm the only newcomer in your life. And an older man. Do they think I'm forty, too?"

"I don't know." She had to press her lips together to keep from smiling. She'd piqued his vanity a bit about his age. "Next time I see them I'll tell them you're only thirty-three."

He cursed under his breath. "Don't do me any favors." He picked up his fly rod and headed up the creek from the pool.

Dina sat on a rock and contemplated the weekend. There was anger in him, but there was passion, too. For her.

She shivered delicately. A delicious lethargy folded around her. It wasn't something she'd consciously considered, but she knew before the weekend was over she would know the passion as well as the anger.

Dina turned the trout over in the skillet. They were perfectly browned. Nonna would have been proud.

Sloan sat at the table, brooding over a can of beer and staring out the window at the last glow of sunset behind the far peaks. He'd made the salads and set the table. She was sautéing the fish in garlic butter and parsley. Microwave-baked potatoes were quartered and browning in the oven with the rolls.

"Ready," she announced, taking the fish filets up. She put everything on a large platter and took it to the table.

Sloan opened a white wine and poured a glass for her. He stayed with his beer.

"This is delicious," he said after taking a bite.

She beamed. "It's the garlic and cinnamon."

"Cinnamon?" He looked doubtful.

"Just a pinch, but your palate knows it's there."

"Your secret ingredient, huh?" His attitude was cynical.

"Yes. What's tweaked your tail this time?" she inquired in conversational tones.

"What makes you think something has?" He practically snarled at her.

"Just the endearing way you snap at anything I say." She gave him a particularly sweet smile.

The silence strummed between them like an unfinished melody while they consumed the meal. Sloan took a slug of beer and slammed the empty can on the table.

Dina flinched, then gave him a reproachful glance.

"Don't," he ordered. "This was a mistake, coming up here with you. I thought I could handle it."

"Handle what?"

"Us. This. I was going to teach you a lesson..." He stopped and gazed out the window some more.

She wanted to shake the words out of him. "What kind of lesson?" Her voice was croakier than ever as she forced the words out. Excitement beat through her like distant drums.

"I was going to make love to you, only...not completely. I was going to reject you and send you scurrying back to Tony."

She felt the hurt he'd meant to inflict. "Why?"

"So you'd realize he was best for you. I don't even know your favorite color."

"Blue. What's yours?"

"Blue." He frowned at her when she smiled. "That doesn't prove a thing. What books do you read?"

"Well, mostly work related. Tax laws and things like that. I have to keep up— What?" she demanded when he scowled.

"So do I. I have to keep up with tax laws, too."

"Well, of course. Let's see, it's my turn to ask something about you. I know. What's one thing you've always wanted to do but haven't had time to learn or try yet?"

"The Iron Man Triathlon. Every year I vow to enter just to see if I can make it."

She gazed at him in surprise. "I'm going to learn to fly one of those ultralight planes."

"Too dangerous. Stick to things on the ground."

"Formula-one racing, then."

He shook his head. "Take one of those defensive driving courses. That'll raise your blood pressure. My instructor put his foot over mine on the accelerator. We took a curve on the outer edges of two wheels. That'll cure you of wanting to go fast and take chances."

"I never get to take chances," she said and sighed. "Someone's always around to yell at me if I do."

"Poor little coddled, spoiled girl."

She wrinkled her nose at him.

"Don't do that."

"What?"

He was staring at her mouth. "Breathe. Talk. Smile." His voice dropped so low she could barely hear him. "I want you."

"I want you, too."

"You're not supposed to say that." His glare was lethal. "You're a traditional woman. You should be planning your wedding and buying your trousseau...and thinking of your wedding night instead of wondering how sex would be with another man...an older man."

She bit her lip to keep it from trembling and looked away from his sudden raw anger. "That was uncalled-for."

He pushed back and went to stand at the sliding glass

door to the patio. "If we make love, it won't mean any-thing. Perhaps if we do, we'll get it out of our systems. Then you can go on with your life."

"What will you do about yours?"

He shrugged. "My life is fine."

"So is mine."

He turned and looked her in the eye. "Is it?"

"Yes."

"Well, mine is hell." He opened the door. "Don't be here when I get back." He stomped out.

She cleaned the kitchen with quick, nervous move-ments, each creak of the house making her jump. After that, she sat in the living room and read a magazine. The wind picked up, and she shivered as the house grew cold.

Sloan didn't return until it was dark. He went directly to the hearth and made a fire. The house began to warm.

He sat on the floor with one knee raised, his arm draped across it, and watched the flames dance over the logs. The glow flickered over him, turning him into a bronzed giant. She longed to touch him, but didn't. At last he sighed and glanced at her.

"I don't understand it," he murmured. "I've known some beautiful women, women who were smart and so-phisticated. It didn't mean a thing. Then I meet you and discover this crazy mix of need and hunger each time I see you or even something that reminds me of you—the scent of a flower, the balm of a sunny day, a bit of laughter in a crowd."

"It isn't my fault," she said defensively, although he hadn't accused her of anything. "I feel it, too."

He spun and rose to his knees in front of her, his face on a level with hers. "I was going to scare you and send you running, but I'm the one who's scared, the one who knows he should be running. Only I can't." He touched her cheek. "Not anymore. It's stronger than I am." His smile was rueful.

His confession moved and confused her. She wanted to comfort him, but she knew to touch him would only add flame to an already explosive situation.

"You'll have to say no," he said softly as he bent to her. He waited, his mouth an inch from hers.

She knew she should, but she couldn't say a word. When he moved again, she closed her eyes and clenched her hands together in her lap. His mouth touched hers.

Their lips merged hungrily, greedily. There was no mercy in the kiss, no tenderness, only need exploding beyond limits. She gave her heart to it, knowing she wouldn't pull back...knowing she was in love, even if he said she wasn't.

"For this moment," she murmured, "I am. For now..."

"Shh." He laid her on the sofa and paused before moving up beside her. "Should I stop?"

"Please don't." She reached for him.

With a groan, he gathered her close and simply held her, rocking them slightly, before he stretched out, his big masculine body covering hers like a protective cloak. She felt safe there. She felt secure.

"I..."

He stopped her with a kiss.

When kissing and caressing weren't enough, he gently removed their clothing item by item until they lay exposed to each other.

"You're incredibly beautiful. I noticed it that day at the cemetery. Lean and strong. I like a woman like that."

"My breasts are small."

"They're perfect." He kissed one, then the other. "Perfect."

She sighed happily and let the dizziness wash all sense of doubt from her. She kissed his throat and his chest, sampled his nipples like a rare new fruit and explored the warmth of muscle and sinew and bone that was him.

"It's wonderful to touch like this," she told him at one point. She gasped as ecstasy seared her in its magic flames.

He grew ever more intimate, bolder with each kiss and caress. She responded in wild, passionate delight.

Once he closed his eyes as if in agony. "How could I ever have thought to withstand this?" He shuddered when she caressed the hard staff that pulsed with life in her hand.

She touched the tip with her finger, then tasted the pearly drop that had collected there. "Come to me."

Sloan sucked in a calming breath and reached for his pants. Her eyes widened slightly, but she didn't ask questions. He prepared himself while she watched, fascinated with everything that was happening between them.

That painful rush of tenderness he'd experienced before with her speared through him. That was another thing between them that he didn't understand. No woman had produced such a confused mix of emotions in him. He didn't like it.

But he didn't dislike it, either.

It was a puzzle wrapped in an enigma within a mystery. And it was damned unsettling. He made one more attempt at reason.

"You should be doing this with Tony."

Something like pain flicked through her eyes, then

was gone. She smiled a wise, knowing, woman's smile. "No, only you."

He sighed and gave up.

Dina held her breath as he moved over her and made a place for himself, his knee nudging her thighs open. She couldn't believe this was going to happen. He was a big man, but she had no fears about making love with him. She'd wanted it too long.

"Don't worry. It'll all go together like a charm."

"I'm not worried at all." She looped her arms around him and sought his mouth, wanting the sweet drugging effect of his kisses and the completeness of being one with him. He kissed her with gentle thrusts of his tongue and the softest persuasion.

He didn't plunge into her like a wild stallion as she half expected. He didn't enter her at all, but slowly began to move, his rigid phallus between her legs, caressing her the way his hands had done earlier. Sensation ran rampant through her.

"Nice," she murmured in surprise.

"Very nice," he agreed, nuzzling her ear.

She sensed his smile, but didn't open her eyes. She couldn't. Everything about her was lethargic, heavy, but tense, too, as need built and began to coil through her.

His bold caresses went on and on. The tension coiled tighter, began to condense and concentrate where he touched her most intimately. She wanted something more...

When she whimpered impatiently, he pressed harder but made no further move. She arched against him.

"That's it. Take what you need. Move. Do whatever you want. You won't hurt me."

She rose to met his every thrust and writhed against him, unable to get enough of the touching, the feel of his body against hers. His hands roamed all over her. He moved one between them and joined the cadence as she strained against him, panting and trembling with needs that had never been this wild.

"Sloan," she whispered, frantic in the kisses she dropped over his chest, frantic in the caresses she gave him, frantic in the surge of power that beat through her. She cried out when the sensations became too great to bear, then burst into a searing pleasure so deep she could feel the contractions rippling through her in wave after wave of sweet release.

And suddenly he was there with her, feeling them, too.

Her lashes were weighted. She forced them open. He was gazing at her. They looked at each other for an eternity.

Then he smiled. And moved.

"Oh," she said.

He moved again, thrusting gently in her. It caused the ripples to start again, a little ping, like a pebble dropped into a stream. Her breathing slowed and deepened.

She ran her hands over his back, liking the feel of his muscles working under the skin as he continued to move slowly. The ripples grew stronger. She looked away from his intent gaze, embarrassed. She wanted it again…that wild pleasure.

"I told you," he murmured softly, laughter in the words.

"Yes, but you didn't say…"

"What?"

"It would be like heaven and earth coming together."

"It'll be like that again."

"Now?" She sounded eager.

"Now," he promised. Still smiling, he kissed her and started the magic all over again.

9

*"*I shouldn't have done that," Sloan said after they'd made love again...and then again.

They were lying in his king-size bed, which was much larger than they needed. They'd slept locked together in the middle of the broad mattress.

"Why?" Dina asked, then covered a wide yawn. She felt wonderful—alive and well and, well, just plain happy.

"Because." He untangled his long limbs from hers and stared at the embers in the hearth.

Sometime during the night, he'd built a fire in the bedroom fireplace at her request. He'd been the gentlest lover. The night had been so incredibly romantic she was still in a daze.

"Because why?" she persisted, ignoring the ping of disappointment that echoed through her.

"I'm your family attorney," he said on such a dismal note that the ping became a full current.

She pushed herself up to one elbow and peered into his eyes. She saw regret, wariness and anger, the latter directed at himself and his lapse of manners, as he apparently saw it.

Flinging the covers back, she sat up, tugging his open pajama top across her breasts. "What an insult," she muttered. "I have the most wonderful experience of my life and *you* regret it. No wonder men get angry when women do that to them. It feels damned awful."

She stomped out of the master bedroom and back to the guest room. Where she should have spent the night.

No. She wasn't going to have regrets. The night had been wonderful. She wasn't going to let regret negate that.

Throwing the pajama top on a chair, she went into the bathroom and took a quick shower, aware of new muscles and a certain tenderness for the first time. Sloan's lovemaking was worth a few aches, she decided fiercely.

And nothing he said could make her think otherwise.

She dressed in the slacks she'd worn to the office the day before and pulled on a long-sleeved cotton sweater in Easter rabbit pink. It matched the glow she felt inside. She packed her overnight case and headed out.

Sloan was in the kitchen. "Breakfast," he announced.

Without speaking, she dropped her things on the sofa and poured herself a cup of coffee. Sloan handed her a plate of bacon and toasted waffles, then prepared one for himself.

Dina smiled with an effort. "Wow," she teased a bit ruthlessly. "Great sex and waffles, too. What could be better?"

He scowled at her.

She took her place at the table. "You don't have to worry. My family won't know what happened. They'll never hear from my lips about how you seduced and ravished me...and gave me such pleasure I still tingle—"

"Knock it off," he ordered gruffly. A lovely shade of red crept up his neck and into his ears.

She was fascinated. "Have I, the country bumpkin, managed to embarrass Mr. Cool from Connecticut?"

"No."

"Then what?"

"I don't want to embarrass you or your family."

She realized he was concerned about her, about what her family would think. She didn't have the excuse of a storm to explain her spending the night with him a second time. There would be lectures, stern ones from Joseph, gently reproving ones from Geoff, concern for her happiness from everyone.

"It's none of their business," she said after a moment of silence. She swallowed. They, like Sloan, would be concerned about her. And they'd blame him.

"It was my fault," he said as if reading her mind.

"It wasn't."

"I'm older. I knew better than to play with fire. I knew what was between us. Instead I—" He didn't say the rest.

"You always do that. It drives me mad."

"Do what?" He eyed her suspiciously.

"Stop before you get to the good part." She arched her brows in mock challenge when he glared at her. He didn't return her playful humor. She sighed and became somber. "So what do you want to do?"

"I'll go talk to your father."

"No."

"Why not?"

She gave him a pitying glance. "Because you would be engaged to me before the conversation was over without quite knowing how it happened. Trust me on this," she advised when his expression turned skeptical.

"Maybe we should become engaged," he said thoughtfully.

Her heart stopped dead still. "Why?"

"It would make things easier for you." He smiled as if he'd solved one of the major problems of the world. "It would get your brothers off your back about Tony. It would please your father..."

"Yes?" She was ready to leap from her chair into his arms.

"Then, after a suitable time, you could break the engagement and say you'd learned your lesson."

She refrained from hitting him with her plate by sheer willpower. "What lesson?" she asked, her jaw so tight she could hardly speak.

"That passion doesn't replace the friendship and respect gained from a long relationship—"

Her chair flew back with a terrible screech when she stood. "You make me so angry, I could...I could... spit...if I weren't such a lady," she announced and walked out, pausing only long enough to grab her purse and two cases from the sofa.

"Wait a minute," he yelled from the door.

She jumped into her car and cranked up the engine. "I'll stop by for you tomorrow afternoon at four."

He headed across the clearing in his sock feet.

Dina took off. "I hope you step on a rock," she muttered, then felt guilty when she saw him wince, then limp a couple of steps before stopping.

She drove on. In the rearview mirror, she saw him raise a hand and wave farewell to her. It gave her the strangest feeling inside. She could really dislike men who thought they had to be gallant and all that.

"I was thinking my black silk," Nonna said, then gazed at Dina to see what she thought.

"That would be lovely with your pink cameo pin and matching earrings," Dina agreed.

"I wanted those to go to you."

"Well..." Dina thought it over. "After the wake, before we go to the cemetery, I can get them. How's that?"

"Good. Take my rings, too. I don't want to be buried in anything grave robbers might want."

"I'm sure no one would bother you—"

"No, no, you take all my jewelry. I saw a news show the other day about grave robbing. Yes," she insisted when Dina looked skeptical. "They attend the funerals to see what people are being buried in, then go back that night and rob them. Imagine their surprise when they don't find anything on me." Nonna cackled like a pleased hen.

"Mama, do you two have to discuss this at the table?" Mr. Dorelli asked.

"It is important," Nonna declared, glaring at her son. "People don't pay respects the way they once did. In my village, we used to sit up three days and nights with the corpse."

"That's because they didn't embalm," Geoff put in. "The wake was to keep animals from eating the body."

"What a delicate way of putting it," Lucien said, eyeing a bite of pink meat on his fork. He put the fork down.

"So, what is this job Nick was telling me about?" her father asked in the ensuing silence.

"It's my own company. That is, I'm a partner in an accounting firm. And it's only three blocks from my apartment."

Her father set his mouth in disapproval. Joseph scowled at her. Nick glared at Joseph. Lucien smiled slightly, but remained silent.

"I am so proud of you," her grandmother stated, then

glanced at the quintet of men as if daring them to dispute her.

There was another beat of silence. All the time she'd helped Lupe and Nonna get Saturday dinner on the table, she'd been worried about being questioned.

"What brings you up to see us this weekend?"

She glanced at her father, then back at her plate. "I, uh, wanted to let you see that I was fine."

"Hmm," her father said.

She instinctively knew he knew she was lying. She wondered if he could tell anything different about her today.

"I saw Sloan Carradine in your car yesterday," Joseph announced in a growl.

"Oh? What were you doing in Denver?" she asked pleasantly, trying to turn the conversation away from her.

"I wanted to see Sloan. You left town with him. I lost you when you got on the freeway."

Every pair of eyes turned to her.

She squared her shoulders. Nothing would make her feel guilty about last night. "Tony called and said you..." She flicked all four of her brothers with an accusing glance. "He said the four of you were going to gang up on Sloan. I simply removed him from harm's way."

Nonna frowned in confusion. "Yesterday, you said? But where did you stay last night?"

In spite of her resolve, Dina felt the heat rush into her face. "At Sloan's cabin, the one where I stayed during the storm, remember?"

"Oh, yes." Her grandmother beamed. "That Sloan. He will make fine babies, yes?"

Geoff choked as he sipped from a glass of iced tea.

Nick pounded him on the back. Joseph turned as red as a steam boiler nearing the exploding point. Her father pressed a hand to his heart. Lucien caught her eye and winked.

Dina gave him a wan smile.

"I will see you in the library after the meal," her father said, his face grim.

Dina nodded. She had only to remain stoic and admit nothing. She was an adult. Her life was her own. She loved her father, but there came a time when he had to let go, too.

When she followed him into the library thirty minutes later, Nonna slipped in, too. She took a seat and picked up her knitting from a basket on the floor. When Joseph entered, her father shook his head. "This is a private meeting."

Joseph glanced at Nonna, then his father. He frowned, but retreated without protest. Dina sighed in relief. Nonna heard and smiled encouragingly at her.

Her father took his seat behind the desk. She sat in one of the wing chairs in front of it. The "hot" seats, she and her brothers had always called them.

"Do I need to speak to Sloan Carradine?" her father asked.

She thought of Sloan's regret for their night together, his guilt at not being able to resist temptation. She shook her head in answer to the question.

The click of Nonna's needles softened the silence.

"I want only your happiness," her father said. He laid a hand to his chest. He'd done that at the dining table, too.

Worry knifed through her. "Papa, are you all right?"

"I'm getting old. Sixty-six next month." He had been the youngest of Nonna's children.

Dina's heart clenched into a painful ball. "You will live to be a hundred and ten." She gave him an affirmative smile as if convincing him of this fact was enough to ensure it.

"I am wondering if I will live to see any grandchildren. Mama, what have I done wrong that none of my children will marry and give us heirs?"

"When they find the right one, they will marry. As you did," she added, her eyes bright with the knowledge of her years. "I think Geoffrey has found his."

"Geoff? Who?" Dina demanded in surprised delight.

"The organist at church."

Dina was disappointed. The woman was older than her brother, and a widow. "Would it be for love or because she would make a suitable preacher's wife?"

Nonna shrugged and went on with her knitting. A smile hovered at the corners of her mouth.

Dina sighed. Love was the most confusing thing. She thought she was in love with Sloan. However, if love was as he said, growing out of a long and steadfast friendship, then she wasn't. She had to be in love with Tony.

And she did love Tony. She knew that. That made her feelings for Sloan all the more confusing. Her feelings for him were nothing like any she'd felt for anyone. She thought of him all the time and longed to have him touch her.

Was she a wanton, a person with no moral fiber? A cheat? A tease? She tried to play fair in her dealings with others. She wished life would play fair with her in return.

"Father, would you please tell your sons to stay away from Sloan? They drew straws to see who would fight him."

"Over you? They wouldn't fight without cause."

The heat rushed to her face. "I told them I couldn't marry Tony because I was, ah, mmm...seeing an older man."

"And they decided it was Sloan," her father concluded.

"Yes."

"I will speak to them." He settled back in the chair. "Sloan is a fine attorney and a practical person. Thoughtful. Intelligent. A good man, I think."

Dina experienced a wave of sadness. "Yes, he's a good man," she agreed soberly.

She'd caused him to forgo his principles. While it hadn't been entirely her fault, she suddenly realized Sloan was a man of honor and it went against his grain to take advantage of their attraction for each other. He felt he should have been the strong one and resisted for both their sakes. Because he was right—she did think intimacy related to love.

"I want you to come look at my shoes," Nonna requested, suddenly breaking into the poignant moment. "Or should I wear any? Perhaps it isn't respectful to have shoes in a casket? That would be like going to bed in them."

"I think you should have shoes for the viewing," Dina told her grandmother, taking her arm and helping her from the chair. "Is your hip bothering you today?"

"Some. It is no matter." Nonna did not believe in giving in to aches and pains.

Dina pushed aside the unhappiness and lifted her chin. Neither would she give in to heartache.

"Would you tell Geoffrey to step in here?" her father called after them. "I'd like to speak to him. Alone."

"Of course. Now someone else is on the hot seat,"

Dina whispered once they were several feet down the hallway.

"Yes." Nonna gave her a conspiratorial smile. "Why do you think I mentioned it?"

"Oh, Nonna." Dina hugged her grandmother, her heart running over with love.

Sloan hardly tasted the dinner placed in front of him. He was at his cousin's home. Clarisse was there, too. Apparently she hadn't found another man in Arizona. She'd also forgiven him, it seemed. He found he really didn't care.

She was sophisticated, mature, cultured, all the things a man would be proud of in a wife.

But she wasn't the woman of his dreams.

That space was reserved for one sexy, skinny woman with a croaky voice and a sharp tongue. And the sweetest mouth and the softest hair and the smoothest skin...

He realized everyone was looking at him. "Beg pardon, what was the question?"

"How you're enjoying your ranch," his cousin supplied.

"Oh, it's...fine, just fine."

"You have some cattle," his cousin prompted.

"Oh, yes. Cattle. Fifty head." He managed an amused drawl. "Guess that makes me a real cowboy of the Wild West."

"We'll have to shop for boots and a ten-gallon hat," Clarisse put in. She touched his arm lightly.

"Oh, and one of those silver belt buckles." This from his cousin's wife.

"Maybe a string tie," his cousin added.

"Nix on the tie," he protested. "This isn't a pedigreed herd. Jeans and a flannel shirt are good enough for 'em.''

And good enough for a certain mountain minx who'd been attracted to him before she'd known he was an attorney. She still didn't realize he came from an old, moneyed family back East. He'd recently inherited a goodly sum from a trust fund set up by his great-grandparents. For Dina, being kin to Nicholas Carradine had been recommendation enough.

He shifted on the tapestry-covered chair as his body went into full arousal at the thought of her. Last weekend had been a mind-blowing experience for him. For her, too. She hadn't tried to hide her delight nor her enthusiasm for his caresses.

"Look at the time," his cousin's wife said, breaking into his reverie. "We don't want to be late at the benefit. After all, it's sponsored by the attorney association."

He helped Clarisse from her chair and draped her stole around her shoulders. She smelled nice, sort of like Dina. Maybe it was the same perfume...

Realizing his thoughts were straying again, he brought them firmly back to safe ground. He was right to leave Dina alone. She was confusing passion with a more lasting emotion. He'd hurt her feelings by voicing his regrets aloud. She should have shared that experience with... He couldn't think of anyone he'd cede those moments to.

He wouldn't take a million dollars for that night with her. It had been all heady delight and discovery, murmurs and laughter and wild excitement...

"Sloan? Coming?"

Everyone was waiting for him while he stood in the foyer in a fog of longing. Heat seeped into his ears.

"You and Clarisse can ride with us," his cousin invited.

He nodded, feeling almost grim, and went out for a gala evening at the opera benefit.

The first voice he heard when they reached their seats was a low, croaky laugh that turned his heart to mush. He turned and there she was, as warm, as radiant, as sunlight on water, wearing a deep golden dress of shimmering silk that reflected the chandeliers in myriad changing hues.

Tony was with her. So was Joseph. Sloan recognized Joseph's date from the Friday night at the Bear Tooth Saloon, but couldn't recall her name.

His gaze was drawn back to Dina. His mountain minx had turned into a butterfly. Her hair was in an old-fashioned roll that bared her slender neck. God, he wanted to kiss her…right there where one curly strand had escaped the pins and nestled against her nape.

She saw him. "Sloan," she called in her friendly way. Her smile dazzled him. "Tony, look, here's Sloan."

Tony leaned over the seat and shook hands with him. So did Joseph. Sloan introduced his cousin and the two women with them.

"Clarisse, I'm happy to meet you. Sloan has spoken of you," Dina said cordially.

Sloan studied her through narrowed eyes. Her smile was perfectly sincere. But then he'd known Dina didn't have a mean or jealous bone in her body.

"Has he?" Clarisse gave Sloan a pleased smile.

He tensed. He didn't want to encourage her. It wasn't that he didn't like her. He did. But like wasn't love.

Love?

He gritted his teeth and forced himself to concentrate

on the conversation and not how luscious Dina looked in that silk dress the color of sunshine.

Finally, the lights dimmed and they all took their seats. Throughout the benefit performance of melodies and arias from the most popular operas, he was totally aware that Dina sat one row behind him. And that she was with another man.

Her oldest and dearest friend, as she'd once described him. The man she should marry. The man who was right for her.

Feeling like a Christian facing the lions, Sloan determined not to interfere in her life. She was better off with Tony. They'd be happy. Have lots of kids, probably.

His body pressed against the restraint of his clothing. He glanced down in annoyance. His jacket kept everything hidden from sight so he looked decent enough. He forced his thoughts from physical longing to practical matters.

Yeah, it was better this way. She'd have a life snug in the bosom of her family, and he'd... He glanced at Clarisse. He'd have a life. He might even marry. Someday.

After meeting with clients on Saturday morning, then having a quick lunch, Dina changed to pink slacks and a pink plaid blouse, which she left open over a white top, before walking over to the cemetery. The weather was perfect for the first day of June—warm and bright. A pleasant breeze stirred the air.

She carried a notepad and paused to read the inscriptions on the tombstones. After roaming the cemetery for an hour, she sat on the granite steps of a mausoleum and contemplated the empty page of the tablet. She couldn't seem to find the right saying to describe Nonna's life.

Nor her own.

Her days seemed as blank as a piece of paper. Seeing Sloan with his date at the benefit last night had driven home to her the futility of longing for that which she couldn't have.

The fact was he didn't love her. He wanted her, but she was not his ideal of the wife he pictured. Clarisse was perfect in every way—older, more experienced, sophisticated. In other words, all the things she wasn't.

Setting her lips firmly together, she put Sloan out of her mind. There were other things in life. Her business was doing well. In fact, she was thinking of hiring an assistant. She got along well with her partner and his wife. Being her own boss was an extra bonus.

So why wasn't she brimming with happiness?

A face appeared in her mental vision. A quiet man with blond hair and blue eyes and the bone structure of the Viking who had surely been one of his ancestors.

Sloan was a thoughtful man who was both tender and fierce when they made love. She could almost feel his mouth on hers.

Lifting her face to the sun, she felt its warm rays like tender needles reaching all the way to her heart. She was wise enough to know the hurt of unrequited love wouldn't last forever, but foolish enough to continue to hope...

With a soul-deep sigh, she ambled along the path to the gate and returned home.

"You have a visitor," Mr. Owens confided with a smile and a teasing wink or two.

Her heart quickened. "Who is it?"

"Run on up and see for yourself." Chuckling, he

went into his living room where his wife read a book. A ball game blared on the television.

Dina walked up the stairs with grave dignity. She was not going to dash up the stairs like an overeager hound hot on the trail of a rabbit.

"Hello?" she called out when she entered her apartment. There was no one in the living room.

"In here," a masculine voice called.

She felt guilty at the disappointment that ran over her. Pressing a smile firmly on her lips, she went into the kitchen. "Nick," she said in pleasant surprise. "What brings you to Denver?"

"I had some business with the sheriff's office. Pop asked me to stop by and tell you to come to Sunday dinner tomorrow. There's some news in the family."

"What?"

"Danged if I know. The old man is being real tight-mouthed over something. He called the rest of the family, too. Everyone will be there." He poured a cup of the coffee he'd brewed in her absence and dug out a fistful of homemade cookies from the crock on the counter.

Dina poured two glasses of milk and sat at the table with her youngest brother, her brow puckered in contemplation.

"Cookie?" he offered.

She took one. "Thanks." She ate it in silence. "What do you think is going on? Are there any clues at all?"

"Not a one, but you know our father. When he gets a flea in his ear, he's unstoppable." Nick looked worried. "I hope he hasn't picked out someone for me."

"Does he know that you...that there's someone—"

He cut her short. "No."

The silence hummed between them while they

downed the snack. Taking their glasses, they went onto the balcony adjoining her bedroom and sat in the shade.

"Can you put me up for the night?" he asked. "We can head out to the ranch around noon."

"Sure." She studied him curiously. "Any reason you want to stay in town? Or are you staying away from home?"

"Can't a fellow want to be with his favorite sister?" he demanded, ruffling her bangs.

She smoothed her hair. "I'm your only sister," she reminded him. "Something's up. What?"

He shrugged. "Nonna told me to have you at the family dinner tomorrow if I had to hog-tie and drag you there."

The hair stood up on her neck. "Didn't she say why?"

"Nope, but it sounds serious. Maybe the pater has decided to disinherit the lot of us. He's pretty mad about the lack of marriage and grandchildren."

"Nonna says Geoff has a gleam in his eye for the organist at church. She's a widow. There's a child, a little boy. I used to have him in nursery class during preaching."

"Ol' Geoff, huh? Yeah, he should get married. A preacher needs a wife."

"I hope that isn't the only reason he's marrying her."

"Don't look so fierce. Geoff wouldn't marry without caring about the person."

"Caring? Is that enough for a marriage to last a lifetime?"

"Who knows?" He eyed her. "You look as if you're losing weight. Are you?"

"I'm pretty busy at work," she said, hedging on the

truth. She often forgot meals in her effort to stay occupied. "Things are easing up now. I'll be able to keep regular hours."

"Good. Nonna is worried about you, I think. She told me you were in love."

Dina's hand jerked, sloshing coffee on her new pink outfit. "When? Why should she think that?" she demanded, patting the drops from her slacks with a tissue.

"Are you in love with Carradine?"

She clenched the mug in both hands. "Why does everyone assume I'm in love with Sloan? There might be someone else in my life. I do know more than one man. And I've dated other men since I've been in town."

"Baxter?" Nick suggested with a knowing grin. "Nah. It's the lawyer who sets your heart to spinning. Joe said you were sad after the benefit show last night."

"Joseph said that?"

"Uh-huh. He notices more than you think."

"I'm not in love with Sloan Carradine," she declared, her jaw tense as she said the words.

"How do you know?"

"He says it's just sex, that we don't know each other well enough to be in love."

Nick started laughing.

Dina frowned, then smiled ruefully at how absurd life, at least the male-female attraction part of it, could become. "It's so confusing," she said.

Nick laughed harder.

10

Sloan stared at the note in his hand as if expecting it to turn into a snake and bite him. It was from Dina's father. The older man had invited him to their home for Sunday dinner at one o'clock. The visit was to be "on tab" as Mr. Dorelli needed his advice on a legal matter—another prenuptial agreement.

A sharp pang whipped through him. Did this mean Dina had agreed to the engagement to Tony, but wanted some changes to the contract?

The pain lodged in his throat, then ricocheted upward, settling into a pounding headache. Would Dina be glad to see him? He'd hurt her by voicing his regrets for taking the passion she should have given her husband.

Oh, for Pete's sake, it wasn't as if passion was something that a person used up and, once it was gone, it was gone. Dina had more than enough for a lifetime.

A funny sensation attacked his chest. He remembered how she'd licked him there, how she'd tasted him and touched him all over and nearly driven him mad with needs he'd hardly known he had. She awakened something urgent and primitive in him.

He forced his mind back to the present. His body throbbed with anticipated pleasure. He glared down at his lap.

"She probably won't be there," he said aloud.

If her father wanted him to do more on the prenuptial agreement, he would refuse, by damn. He'd had enough of the Dorelli family and their interference in each other's lives. He'd go to the blasted dinner, but he'd tell them he was resigning as their attorney. That would release him from any obligation to talk sense into Dina.

He tossed the note into the trash can and turned toward the window. The mountains loomed like stolid mastiffs on the horizon, watching over the city, guarding its citizens. He wondered what she was doing this Saturday afternoon. Working as he was?

"Sloan, I'm outa here," his cousin said, sticking his head around the door. "You want to come over to dinner tonight? Nothing fancy. I'm going to grill steaks."

Sloan glanced at the trash can. "Anyone else coming?"

His cousin pushed the door all the way open and propped his shoulders against the frame. "Such as Clarisse?"

"Yeah."

"Probably. She practically lives at our house these days."

Sloan decided to be candid. "I hate to pass on free steak, but I don't think I'll come."

A moment passed. Robby rubbed a finger over his bottom lip. "You know, I think I'll have a talk with the little woman about her best friend. I'm getting damned tired of stepping around Clarisse to see my wife."

"Good idea," Sloan agreed. He exchanged a glance of understanding with his cousin.

"Meet anyone interesting of late?" Robby asked casually.

Sloan glanced toward the trash can again.

"What the hell is in there?" Robby demanded.

Sloan looked a question his way.

"The trash can. You keep glancing at it as if expecting Mary Poppins to appear."

"An invitation to dinner at the Dorelli place tomorrow."

Robby considered the implications and the undertone in his cousin's voice. "You hot for the Dorelli girl?"

"Elegantly put, cuz," Sloan drawled. "If I am?" He waited to see what kind of advice his cousin would give.

"She's got four older brothers. Big bruisers for the most part. You'd better watch yourself if you're thinking of getting mixed up with her."

Sloan smiled sardonically. "I hear you."

Robby cocked his head to one side and studied his cousin. "I think I hear a *but* at the end of that statement. Should it be—I hear you, but the advice is too late?"

"Something like that."

Robby's eyes widened. "You really are mixed up with her?"

"Sort of," Sloan admitted. *Hell.* He was so totally mixed up with her, over her, around her, he couldn't think straight.

"Boy, you're in a heap o' trouble. Her old man already picked out the groom for her."

"Fiobono Cheese."

"Right. The two go together like cows and milk."

"Dina isn't a cow to be auctioned off. She's left the family home and business and lives here in the city."

Robby's eyebrows shot up to the crisp wing of tawny hair that swept over his forehead. "That must have caused some fallout on the home front. Those old Italian families have been here since the gold rush. They tend to hang close with each other. You did some work for the senior Dorelli recently, didn't you?''

''Yes. A prenuptial agreement for the Dorelli daughter and the Fiobono son. The daughter refused to go along. As the family lawyer, I talked to her about the advantages. She's known Tony all her life. It would be a sound match.'' He looked toward the wastebasket and the invitation lying in it.

''Hmm,'' Robby said with a sly gleam in his eyes. ''Are you going to the dinner?''

''Yes.'' He made up his mind at that moment.

''I envy you. The old grandma cooks like a dream. She used to send homemade rolls and bread to us when her son came to town. Our great-uncle was in love with her.''

''Nicholas?''

''Just kidding. She was married, of course, and evidently in love with her husband, but there was a spark between them.'' He pushed himself off the frame. ''I'm going to beat Brody at tennis today. Then I think I'll go home and make love to my wife...before I tell her to tell her best friend to get lost.''

''Good luck,'' Sloan called after him.

The office was deadly silent after the other man left. Sloan glanced around the room. The ficus tree was doing nicely. So were the other plants he'd added. But the place still didn't have the vibrancy of Dina's office.

Because she wasn't there?

He tried to read a report, but couldn't. He couldn't get her out of his mind. What had happened to his self-discipline?

Where Dina Dorelli was concerned he had none.

Dina chose her favorite pink linen suit with a white lace blouse for the dinner with her family. She made two thin braids at each temple and pulled them up to meet on top of her head. She clipped them together with a pink lace butterfly.

"Nice," her brother approved, coming out of her bedroom where he'd confiscated her shower and toilet articles before dressing in his casual clothes again.

"It feels odd going to the ranch as if I'm a guest instead of the daughter of the house."

"Nonna will put you to work helping her and Lupe as soon as you walk in the door."

She smiled, feeling nostalgic. "Yes. I made dozens of egg noodles last weekend."

"For the big family get-together today." Nick buttoned his shirt. "Ready?"

She nodded and stood. With white pumps and purse and her good suit, she felt ready to face her aunt, uncle, their spouses and the cousins again. "What do you suppose Papa is up to?"

"Dunno. I suppose we'll soon find out." Nick held the door to her car before climbing in his truck and following her to the highway.

At her house, Nonna met them at the door. She gave Nick a buss on the cheek and sent him into the family room where a ball game was in progress. "Come into the kitchen," she told Dina after kissing her on each cheek.

"Something smells wonderful," Dina remarked. She hung her jacket in the closet and laid her purse on the sideboard before joining her grandmother and Lupe in the huge kitchen. "What shall I do?"

"Make the salad," Nonna ordered.

"It's done. The cake needs icing," Lupe contradicted.

Dina tossed the loop of an apron over her head and tied the strings behind her. She got out the powdered sugar and butter.

The next hour passed in contented industry. Dina loved being in the kitchen with the other two women. Bonds, she thought. Family ties. Tears burned her eyes.

At twelve-thirty, cars started arriving as other family members came straight over from church. Voices she'd known since birth called out greetings. Her aunt came into the kitchen followed by Miss Pettibone, the book-keeper for the dairy.

"Geoffrey let us out early today. He must have been hungry," her aunt told them. She gave Dina a kiss on each cheek. "You look like the first rose of summer. Is that a new suit?"

"Yes."

"That pink is all the rage this year. You see it everywhere," Aunt Rosie informed them, taking off her jacket and hitching an apron over her head and around her ample waist before joining them in preparing the meal. "Miss Pettibone, you look nice, too. Is that a new outfit?"

"Yes, it is." Miss Pettibone wore a pale peach dress with long sleeves and lace at the neck. She had on pearl earrings. Her hair had been newly permed into a delicate white fluff around her face. She looked very pretty with her fair skin and blue eyes. Her cheeks were slightly flushed.

How I love them, Dina admitted, casting an affectionate eye over her relatives, and the cook and bookkeeper who'd been with them for years. She listened while news and gossip were exchanged and answered when asked about her new job. She was quiet, enjoying the sounds of their voices, her heart so filled with love it hurt.

The cousins arrived, popped their heads into the kitchen to say hi, then disappeared. She heard her father's voice among the others. He greeted someone, then she heard the other answer.

"Sloan," she muttered, her heart all but stopping. Heat rushed from someplace deep inside her and washed over her in a tidal wave of emotion too strong to be ignored.

"Yes, your father asked him to come today in case he was needed."

"Why…" She cleared the croak from her throat. "Why would Papa need an attorney?"

"I don't know. He wouldn't say." Nonna cast a dark glance of irritation toward the front hall and the masculine voices. "I should mention my will to Sloan. I want to make sure they know Nicholas drew one up for me before he retired."

"Old Mr. Carradine died," Lupe interjected in her practical manner. "Right at his desk. He had heart-dropsy."

"He didn't," Nonna retorted. "It was a heart attack."

"His heart went arrhythmic," Dina explained.

"Heart-dropsy," Lupe said as if Dina had confirmed it.

"A heart attack," Nonna insisted.

"Is everything ready to take to the table?" Aunt Rosie hurriedly put in.

Nonna directed them in setting the long table capable of seating sixteen easily. Each side had nine plates and an extra chair squeezed in with the regular dining chairs. Dina's heart went *thumpety-thunk* and sank to her toes.

Coward, she scoffed at herself. Lifting her chin, she carried the bowls of homemade noodle soup with tiny liver dumplings in and set them on the service plates.

"Dinner is ready," Aunt Rosie announced.

There was a general shuffling as the men went to wash their hands—or risk a lecture from Nonna if they forgot—then came to the long table. Sloan entered the dining room with her father.

Determined not to be intimidated by his masculine presence, she smiled his way and went on with her task. She couldn't quite bring herself to look into his eyes.

"Save me a seat," she whispered to Nick.

He gave her a quizzical glance. Her place was on the other side of the table, by the end where Nonna presided. She returned to the kitchen for the last two bowls of soup and followed Aunt Rosie carrying the baskets of rolls back to the dining room. Her aunt took her usual place. Miss Pettibone was seated next to her father. That left only one spot for Dina.

Nick shot her an apologetic glance and shrugged. Dina sat in the empty chair next to Sloan.

Everyone joined hands while Geoffrey gave the blessing.

Dina ignored her heart when Sloan's large hand closed over hers, but she couldn't ignore the heat lightning that jolted from him to her, settling like a coil of radiant energy in her middle.

The blessing droned on forever. She pulled her hand free before the amen was hardly spoken.

"Isn't this the loveliest weather?" her aunt started the conversational ball rolling.

Her father agreed that it was, sounding as ebullient as Uncle Bert. In fact, everything about her father was more...more...*everything* today. His smile was bright, his eyes twinkled, his demeanor was one of self-satisfaction.

An inner alarm clanged.

A cousin asked Nick something about fishing. Uncle Bert asked Joseph about some new medicine for pinkeye for the cows. Aunt Rosie talked to Uncle Bert's wife about the latest baby in the neighborhood. Dina was acutely conscious of Sloan.

"Hello," he said in his attractive baritone, leaning slightly toward her.

"Hello. How are you?" she asked pleasantly. She'd be dignified and civil if it killed her.

"I'm not sure." His smile was rueful. "It's been a damned difficult week. I keep remembering things I shouldn't."

Her eyes met his. A wild blush ran over her entire body, no matter that she'd told herself when she sat down that she wasn't going to react to anything about him.

"You know what we nearly forgot?" Nonna interrupted, placing a bony hand to her heart.

"What?" Dina asked, blinking as she tried to tune Sloan out and her grandmother in.

"Music. What do you think we should have?"

Dina looked at her blankly, unable to relate to the question.

"For my service," Nonna added impatiently. "Maybe you'd sing something soft and pretty."

"You'd better opt for 'Down in the Valley,' then," Nick suggested cheerfully. "That's the only song she can sing without sounding like a scalded cat."

Sloan looked from Nonna on his right at the end of the table to Dina at his left and Nick directly across from him. Dina had to grin. He wasn't following the conversation.

"Nonna is preparing for her funeral," she reminded him. "Remember? I was looking at tombstones that day in the cemetery where we met."

"Oh, yes."

"'O, Holy Night' is my favorite," Nonna confided, "but that's a Christmas song."

"You should have whatever music you like best." Dina flashed Sloan a glance that dared him to deny it.

Sloan nodded in agreement. Something tender sprang up in him. She was so fiercely loyal to those she loved.

A man could go far and not find a woman half so...so...what? He couldn't think of a word to define her. Wonderful? Nah. She was stubborn and opinionated. She did what she damned well pleased. She drove him crazy with her croaky laughter, her sexy walk, her smart mouth...which he wanted to kiss right now, this very moment.

She leaned past him and suggested a hymn to her grandmother.

"Yes, definitely that one. Write it down," Nonna ordered. "Did you look at any of the cemeteries in Denver?"

"Yes, but I couldn't find anything."

"I'm getting worried. I need to decide soon."

"Nonna, you're only ninety-three. We have plenty of time," Dina chided. "Your family lives to be a hundred."

Seven more years, Sloan thought. A jab of pain hit him. Dina would miss her grandmother when the old lady was gone. She would need someone to comfort her.

Right. That would be her husband's job. He stirred uneasily on the tapestry-covered chair as visions came to him. Dina married. Dina big with child...busy with her baby...sharing her heart, all of her love, with a husband.

He watched the others during the long, noisy meal. There were undercurrents in the air. Mr. Dorelli looked too pleased not to have some news to impart. And there was the fact of his own presence, requested in case his legal services were needed.

Tony and his father weren't present. Surely there wasn't going to be an engagement announced. But Dina had looked pretty happy Friday night at the benefit. So had Tony.

His uneasiness increased.

At last the meal was finished with bowls of pudding and cream sauce. Just as Sloan relaxed, Mr. Dorelli raised his wineglass and signaled for quiet.

Sloan felt his heart race, then skip, then race again. An adrenaline rush broke out a sweat all over his body. He didn't know whether he was preparing to fight or run.

"I have an announcement to make," Mr. Dorelli said with an expansive smile. He glanced down the table, pausing at each face as if assessing the thoughts behind the expressions.

Sloan laid his spoon down and clenched his fist in his lap.

"There is to be a marriage in the family, after all." Mr. Dorelli became very serious. His eyes lingered on Dina for a second, then moved on, past him to the old lady at the end of the table. "I hope you will bless this union, Mama," he said. He raised his glass. "I give you—"

"No," Sloan said.

Every eye turned to him, shock in some, curiosity in others.

He stood and faced Mr. Dorelli. "Dina will marry no one but me." He turned a fierce glance on her. *"Me,"* he told her in a tone that said he meant business.

Her lovely face went as pink as her skirt.

"You may make your announcement after mine," her father scolded. "I started first."

Sloan took a deep breath and prepared his opening argument. "She can't marry Tony. She doesn't love him...well, she does, but as a brother or cousin or something, not as a husband. Not the way she loves me," he added softly, turning to her. He watched the color climb right to her hairline. "He doesn't love her, not the way I do." He paused. "I do love you, you know," he said, bending slightly toward her.

She looked up at him, her face somber. For once, she didn't have a smart comeback. He smiled. The tender shoot of love curled around and around his heart, wrapping it in love for her, this woman who brought him warmth and laughter and passion.

His grip on her arm tugged her upright. They faced each other. The family looked on in rapt attention. Lupe stood at the doorway to the kitchen, her mouth agape.

"You have to marry me," he said, going into his closing statement. "I'm miserable without you. Each day is longer than the one before. I think of you all the time. I dream of you. I miss you."

"Sloan," she said softly, his name going up, breaking, then ending in a choky gurgle.

He smiled. "Keep saying my name like that for the next fifty years and I'll be a happy man."

"I will." It was a promise.

Sloan relaxed a tad.

She tilted her head to gaze past Sloan to her father. He was watching them with a stern expression. "I love him, Papa. I want to marry Sloan."

Sloan took her hand and turned to face the patriarch of the family. "We would like your blessing, sir." He waited tensely for the old man to reply. Dina's hand trembled in his.

"Well, I suppose you'd marry anyway, whether I give it or not," he grumbled.

Sloan stoically faced the frown. He put an arm around Dina's shoulders, hating that she might be hurt because of her love for him. "Yes, we will."

"Yes," Dina echoed.

"Give them your blessing and put them out of their misery," Nonna ordered from the end of the table.

Mr. Dorelli surprised them with a smile. "You have my blessing." He raised his glass to them, then drank.

The four brothers and five cousins cheered, laughter and talk broke out all around them. Sloan, unable to resist, thought the occasion called for a kiss. He slipped a finger under Dina's chin and placed a quick but tender kiss on her mouth.

Longing spread through him. He wished they were alone.

"Now will you two sit down so I can get on with my news?" Mr. Dorelli demanded.

Sloan and Dina sat.

"Now." Mr. Dorelli lifted his glass once more. "We will be adding a new—" he glanced at Sloan "—another new member to the family."

Dina looked at Geoff. He didn't look like a happy, newly engaged man. He watched their father with his usual benign smile. Lucien raised and dropped his shoulders to show he didn't know what was going on when she looked at him. So did Nick. Joseph wore a troubled frown, so she didn't think it was him.

"Camilla has agreed to become my wife," Papa said. "We would like to be married right away. We are not so young as others. We ask your blessings." He looked at his mother.

Nonna laid a hand over her mouth. "You...and Miss Pettibone?" she finally asked.

"Her name is Camilla," Mr. Dorelli said with dignity.

"Camilla," Nonna repeated.

Dina gave her grandmother a little kick under the table.

"You have my blessing, my son," the old woman said with grave courtesy. "I wish you happiness."

Sloan lifted his glass. "Happiness," he repeated.

Dina was grateful for his gesture. The rest of the family followed suit, toasting her father and his future bride, who looked a bit uncertain now that the announcement was made.

Dina's heart went out to the woman. She knew how it felt to think you might not be wanted. She cast Sloan a sideways glance. They had a lot to talk over. She frowned. In fact, he had a lot of explaining to do, jumping in like that and saying she was in love with him in front of her whole family without so much as a word to her—

"Don't get in a miff," he whispered, as if reading her mind.

When she looked into those sky blue eyes, she melted like strawberry ice cream in the sun.

"I was desperate," he continued. "I thought...well, never mind. We'll talk later. Will you come to my place after we get through here? We can stay the night and drive in to the city in the morning. I think we'll be up early.''

She restrained herself from kissing the grin right off his face in front of everyone. She nodded.

It was almost dark before the gathering started to break up.

"He will give you strong, healthy children," Nonna said to Dina, speaking in Italian. "Don't wait too long. I want to see at least one bambino before I die."

"In nine months," he replied.

Dina stared up at him. "You speak Italian?"

"No, Spanish, but I understand quite a bit." He glanced at his thumbs and grinned.

Dina noticed Nonna's red face. "Serves you right for saying such things."

Laughing, they kissed on each cheek. Nonna stood on the porch and waved them off.

Sloan and Dina left, each in a car. She followed him to his ranch cabin. He helped her out of the car and looped an arm around her as they walked to the door. Their hips bumped. Their pulses raced. They both wore grins.

"That Nonna," Dina said.

"Yes," he said huskily.

She fell silent when they entered the lovely cabin and stopped in the middle of the living room.

"I think we'd better talk," he said, guiding them to the sofa. He pushed her gently into the cushions and took a seat beside her, his arm around her as if he couldn't let her go.

"I was so shocked..." She shook her head.

"I thought your father was going to announce your engagement to Tony. I couldn't let you marry him, not when you're in love with me."

"How did you know? I wasn't sure myself until last week."

"I realized the feeling between us was too strong to be only passion. Last weekend blew my mind. I kept thinking about it, about us, all week, about why it was different between us."

"The passion?"

He kissed her nose, then her mouth for a long time. "Don't distract me," he warned. "Yes, the passion. And the laughter. The good feeling of sleeping with you, of waking with you. The wonder of it all. I couldn't figure it out."

"When did you, um, know how you felt?"

"For sure?"

She nodded.

"Today. Seeing you, all I could think about was kissing you. When I thought I might have lost you because of my stupidity—"

"Your sense of responsibility," she corrected, giving him a fierce glance. "And your past. Passion hadn't been a lasting emotion from your experiences. You thought you had to do what was in my best interest." She smiled. "Which you are."

"Yes," he agreed. "I'll love you as long as I live. I want you with me forever. I think you're beautiful, even if you do sound like a frog. Is this getting sappy enough for you?" he inquired with a quiver of laughter in his voice.

She gave him an exasperated grimace. "You were doing fine up to the frog part."

He caught her to him. "Croak for me. The first thing you need to say is yes."

"Yes," she said with a lovely croak. "When?"

"Two weeks? Is that enough time? I want a June

bride. That's all I can wait.'' He set her carefully away from him.

She leaned on him, elbows propped sharply on his chest. "I can't wait another second. Kiss me.''

"Don't tempt me, Dina. I'm trying to be honorable about this.''

"Ha! on your honor,'' she scoffed and tried to kiss him, hitting his chin when he jerked away.

"We need to be sensible. Let go of my tie. What are you doing? Dammit, you tore off a button. Stop that! You little devil! Ouch!''

"Kiss me or I'll bite you again.'' She had her hands on him now, roaming his bare skin. She sighed and licked his chest, then sucked at his nipple.

"Let's take these clothes off,'' he muttered.

"I thought you'd never get around to it.''

11

Dina lay back against the pillow with a sigh. She tucked her gown into place again. Sloan held their three-day-old daughter to his shoulder and patted her back. When she burped, he grinned as if he'd just knocked a home run at the World Series.

Nonna bustled in. "How is our bambina?" she asked.

Sloan handed the baby over. Nonna made clucking noises.

Dina watched them, a lazy river of love running through her heart. Her family. Husband, child and grandmother.

When Nonna had moved down to the cottage with Joseph and Lucien, declaring three women were too many in one house, her brothers had been slightly dismayed. She'd put them on a weekend curfew, expecting them home by midnight so she could get to sleep. Sloan had solved the dilemma. He'd invited her to live with them.

"Can I feed her?" a feminine voice demanded from the door.

Dina smiled at their other daughter, three-year-old Niccole Amelia, named for Nicholas Carradine and her brother. Amelia was for Nonna. "She just ate."

Nikky frowned. "When do I get to feed her?"

"When she needs some water, I will let you take care of her," Nonna promised. "Come, let's put this one in bed. She's sleeping like a lamb. Then we will read stories."

"Nonna, I have something for you," Sloan mentioned, stopping her exit. He held out a slip of paper so she could read it without disturbing the baby.

"'To live in the hearts of those you love is never to die,'" she read aloud.

"What do you think?" he asked.

"Do you like it, Nonna?" Nikky piped up.

They waited anxiously for the answer. She read it again. She thought it over. A smile broke out on her face. "'To live in the hearts of those you love...'" she repeated. She glanced at Dina, at Sloan, at Nikky and the new baby. She sighed happily, contentedly. "Perfect. Yes. This is it. Exactly what I want."

Dina started laughing. Sloan joined in.

So did Nikky. She didn't exactly understand the laughter, but it was often that way in her family. Her mother would laugh, then her father. Grown-ups were funny that way.

Yeah, they were.

She nodded to herself and skipped to keep up. She followed Nonna into the baby's room. Behind her, the laughter changed to silence. She knew the why of that. Her father was kissing her mom. They did that a lot, too.

Yeah, they did.

* * * * *

FOR BETTER . . . FOR WORSE . . .
FOR A WEEK

**The seven days that turned two couples'
lives topsy-turvy!**

A darling Yours Truly duet by
HAYLEY GARDNER

THE ONE-WEEK WIFE
June 1997

A baby left on a doorstep...which results in a
one-week battle-of-the-sexes bet on whether
a man or a woman can take better care of
little Teddy. All's fair in war...and love!

THE ONE-WEEK BABY
July 1997

A pretend wife for a week...which results in
a next-door-neighbor romance that is
anything but neighborly. Pretending isn't half
as much fun as the real thing....

Heat up your summer with short,
sassy love stories from
Hayley Gardner and Yours Truly.
Romance has never been hotter!

This summer, the legend
continues in Jacobsville

Diana Palmer

A LONG, TALL TEXAN SUMMER

Three **BRAND-NEW** short stories

This summer, Silhouette brings readers a special
collection for Diana Palmer's LONG, TALL TEXANS
fans. Diana has rounded up three **BRAND-NEW**
stories of love Texas-style, all set in Jacobsville,
Texas. Featuring the men you've grown to love from
this wonderful town, this collection is a must-have
for all fans!

*They grow 'em tall in the saddle in Texas—and
they've got love and marriage on their minds!*

Don't miss this collection of original Long, Tall Texans
stories...available in June at your favorite retail outlet.

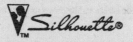

Look us up on-line at: http://www.romance.net   LTTST

And the Winner Is...
You!

...when you pick up these great titles
from our new promotion at your
favorite retail outlet this June!

Diana Palmer
The Case of the Mesmerizing Boss

Betty Neels
The Convenient Wife

Annette Broadrick
Irresistible

Emma Darcy
A Wedding to Remember

Rachel Lee
Lost Warriors

Marie Ferrarella
Father Goose

HARLEQUIN ® 🔻 *Silhouette*®

As seen on TV!
Free Gift Offer

With a Free Gift proof-of-purchase from any Silhouette® book,
you can receive a beautiful cubic zirconia pendant.

This gorgeous marquise-shaped stone is a genuine cubic
zirconia—accented by an 18" gold tone necklace.

(Approximate retail value $19.95)

Send for yours today...
compliments of ▼ *Silhouette*®

To receive your free gift, a cubic zirconia pendant, send us one original proof-of-
purchase, photocopies not accepted, from the back of any Silhouette Romance™,
Silhouette Desire®, Silhouette Special Edition®, Silhouette Intimate Moments®
or Silhouette Yours Truly™ title available in February, March and April at your favorite
retail outlet, together with the Free Gift Certificate, plus a check or money order for
$1.65 U.S./$2.15 CAN. (do not send cash) to cover postage and handling, payable
to Silhouette Free Gift Offer. We will send you the specified gift. Allow 6 to 8 weeks for
delivery. Offer good until April 30, 1997 or while quantities last. Offer valid in the
U.S. and Canada only.

Free Gift Certificate

Name: _____

Address: _____

City: _____ State/Province: _____ Zip/Postal Code: _____

Mail this certificate, one proof-of-purchase and a check or money order for postage
and handling to: SILHOUETTE FREE GIFT OFFER 1997. In the U.S.: 3010 Walden
Avenue, P.O. Box 9077, Buffalo NY 14269-9077. In Canada: P.O. Box 613, Fort Erie,
Ontario L2Z 5X3.

FREE GIFT OFFER   084-KFD
ONE PROOF-OF-PURCHASE
To collect your fabulous FREE GIFT, a cubic zirconia pendant, you must include this
original proof-of-purchase for each gift with the properly completed Free Gift Certificate.

084-KFD

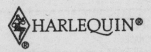